I0729856

The Keepers of Time

Into the Vortex of Shadows

Elizabeth Chappelle

HUMMINGBIRD
PUBLISHING LTD

Hummingbird Publishing Ltd

Paperback-978-1-78520-155-4

Contents

Synopsis

Aurelius nodded, overwhelmed but determined to uncover the truth, he confronted the man who had taken him from his family, then everything went dark, and all had been forgotten as if his memory had been wiped clean.

The journey that followed was filled with moments of revelation and reunion after the man who took him, died, they had to try to reconnect with him in a different way, but along that journey he had meet Sereena, Xavier and Rebecca/Stella each one filling in the missing pieces of his past. The tattoo on his wrist, a symbol of his heritage, was a constant reminder of his identity.

Chapter 1

L ife had never been the same, filled with love, excitement, passion, commitment and strength, he still remembered the victims even though going back in time to stop Liber and save the first and future women. He had learnt the women were from the future, their encounter with Liber was just pure chance. His love for Aurora was strong, taking them back through time was to get notice, sending a message, but did not anticipate that they would die in the process. He panicked, he couldn't stop, he wanted to be stopped, but didn't know how. At the time Aurelius did not care about the reason, he still felt anger at the thought. It had been five years since Liber had been caught in nineteen ninety-three timeline, Chief Martin Peters/Aurelius felt a sense of achievement the day, he was caught, the whole case had haunted him for some time, until that day, the day Catherine and his unborn son was alive, and the timeline was saved and reset as well as him finding out his identity. His life had changed. Life was hectic with a four-year-old, but Chief Martin Peters/Aurelius was loving his life. Everyday his heart warmed as he looked into his son's bright eyes and innocent smile Caius's laughter was like a soothing balm, washing away the stress of the day. Despite the chaos, a profound sense of contentment resided in his heart, the joy of fatherhood filled him with a purpose he had never known before. Balendin, Sereena, his father Xander, Leo and Xavier were frequent visitors, ensure all was well, the sad part was he had not told Catherine of who he really is and who his family were.

Aurelius heart still ached as memories from his childhood slowly resurfaced, reminding him of how much he had missed, his mother, Aurelia. He slowly remembered part of her face, her sweet sent. The memories were a complex blend of happiness and sorrow, vivid images of laughter intertwined with tears of love and loss. He could almost feel the gentle touch of her hand, the warmth of her embrace, and hear the soothing sound of her voice singing to him to sleep. These memories were like a balm to his soul, yet they also brought a stinging pain, knowing that those moments were forever lost in time. He carried a photo her that Balendin and his father gave him to help him remember things.

On Xyphoria Prime they had technology that video special events that were stored in a memory bank. Aurelius had gone to Xyphoria Prime a few times to see his once home, Balendin and his father would spend hours showing the replays, but some of it Aurelius did not recall those events, it would leave his heart aching as he longed to feel his mother's touch again and felt if he had listened to them the day in Central Parks and gone with them instead of confronting the man that stole him he would of seen her and been with her before she died.

The citizens were warm and friendly, the older generation that still looked young would often fill in gaps and tell stories of how mischievous he was, but the most important thing was how kind he was and generous.

His heart felt heavy and would often find himself standing at the window staring out into the vast expanse of the sky, lost in thought. He longed to share those memories with Catherine to tell her the truth about who he is and to show her his home Xyphoria Prime, but fear held him back, the fear of how she might react, the fear of losing the life they had built together. The thought of her leaving, taking Caius with her was unbearable the pain was too great. His mind was a whirlwind of emotions, oscillating between the desire for honesty and the fear of its consequences.

Chapter 2

Aurelius arrived home from the precinct, returning home to him the best part of the day, where could be with his family, his mind still occupied with the day's events. As he stepped through the door, he was greeted by the familiar sounds of Caius's laughter and the aroma of Catherine's cooking. He felt a sense of peace wash over him, a stark contrast to the chaos of his work life.

"Daddy!" Caius excitable yelled, as he come running up to him with open arms.

Aurelius scooped him up, smiling, "Hey, how was your day?"

Caius continued about his day, as soon as he mentioned the fountain, Aurelius heart missed a beat, he hadn't thought about Xyphoria for a while as the thought made him long for him to be there.

Aurelius casually laughed, as he settled him down, "That's sounds wonderful."

Just as he was about to join Catherine in the kitchen, there was a knock on the door, Aurelius's stopped short, it was unusual hour for visitors. Exchanging a curious glance with Catherine before heading to the door.

Upon opening it, he found Balendin standing there, his expression grave, "Balendin, what brings you here?" Aurelius asked as he is step aside to let him in.

Balendin's eyes filled with a mix of fear and sadness, "Aurelius, I need your help." Balendin stopped in midsentence trying to compose himself. Bowing his head gathering his thoughts he continued, "It's Sereena, she been kidnapped?"

Aurelius felt a chill run down his spine, "How? By whom?"

With his voice shaking slightly replied, "We don't know yet, she was on her return to Xyphoria Prime." His voice tone become panicky, "We need to find her, she is in grave danger."

Catherine appeared at the doorway, "Who's been kidnapped? Sereena?"

Aurelius turned to her, his expression somber, "Sereena, she was taken on route to home." As soon as he said home, he realized, Xyphoria was home.

Catherine's eyes widened with a mix of fear, she know this was his job this is who he is, feeling her anxiety come over her as she realized how closed to home this was. As far as Catherine know Sereena worked with Aurelius.

Balendin heart felt a warm glow as he realized just how much family do stick together, wiped a tear as he looked at Aurelius, "It might be dangerous, we don't know who or where she is."

Aurelius was no stranger to danger and had had a strong desire, "Alright, together we find her." He paused, thinking of one person who could provide the guidance they need, "We'll need help and we know just one person, her abilities as a medium could be crucial."

Balendin nodded as he tried to fight his tears, Aurelius hugged him, his soothing voice reassuring him, "It will be alright, we will find her and bring her home."

Balendin upon those words he could not contain his tears any longer, he had not cried like that since his brother had been taken. He trusted Aurelius and knew what when he said 'it will be okay,' it would indeed be the case.

The evening seamed long, Balendin stayed the night as could not face leaving as very emotional and needed his brother. Aurelius got up early to catch Isabel, which without hesitation agreed, her presence brought a sense of comfort and hope as they prepared for the journey back to Xyphoria Prime, and besides, she had never been there before, he had to brief her.

The trip felt longer than it was, filled with mixture of dread and anticipation, he eyes betraying the worry that he tried to hide. Aurelius sat beside him his hand resting on his shoulders providing silent support.

Eventually arriving on the planet, they were greeted by Xavier, Daniels, now known as Leo, which seemed fitting name for him, and Xander. The reunion was tense, the urgency of the situation hanging heavy in the air.

Aurelius's voice was steady but filled with emotion, "We need to find out what happened,"

Xavier, his face drawn with worry, spoke up, "We have some leads, but nothing concrete, but we need to discuss our option and come up with a plan."

As they gather in a secure location, the atmosphere charged with anxiety, Balendin's eyes were dark with worry, his love for Sereena driving him forward. He knows all too well from experience, how crucial it is to find them, "We need to act fast, every moment we waste is another moment she's in danger."

Isabel got straight to work, closing her eyes, she tried to channel but something dark and malevolent was blocking her. She tried to break through an image appeared, she whispered, "He has markings all over his body." It suddenly dawns on her where she has seen those makings before, Liber had the same, "He's connected to Liber."

The colour drained from Balendin's and Aurelius's faces as Liber's name was mentioned, Balendin and Xavier instantly know who she was referring to, together they said "Icarus, she's on Zamathia Vortex!"

Xander placed a reassuring hand on Balendin's shoulder, "We'll find her, son, we won't stop until she is safe."

Isabel shouted, "Wait! She's here."

The room was filled with a flurry of activity as they coordinated their efforts, Aurelius's heart ached for Balendin, knowing that pain of missing someone you love. He caught Isabel's eye, her expression mirroring his own emotions. They prepared to move out, Aurelius had a surge of resolve, they had a plan and they had each other, together they would find Sereena and bring her home.

Aurelius, Balendin and Isabel headed towards the outskirts of city, Isabel suddenly stopped, her eyes wide, "She's close, I can now feel her presence."

Balendin's heart raced, "Where?"

Isabel pointed towards the forest near the mountains, Aurelius and Balendin raced towards the forest and slowly approach an old, abandoned building, "In there."

Aurelius took the lead, his senses on high alert, they entered the building, the air was thick with tension, as they moved silently, their eyes scanning every shadow.

They heard muffled cry coming from one of the rooms, "Sereena." Balendin whispered, his voice breaking as he followed the sound, his heart pounding as he turned the corner, he saw Sereena tied to the table, her eyes widen with fear and standing beside her stood a figure, his face twisted with malice.

"Let her go," Aurelius command, his voice steady but fierce.

The figure laughed a cold, chilling sound, "Why would I do that?"

Balendin clenched his fists, "If you don`t, you`ll regret it."

The figure made a growling sound as they spoke, "I doubt that."

Sizing the opportunity Aurelius moved quickly and in a swift, decisive move he knocked the figure to the ground, the figure crackled a laugh as he held them down, then he suddenly vanished, Aurelius looked confused, "Where did he go?"

Balendin rushed to Sereena, untying her bonds, lifting her into his arms, his emotions overwhelmed him as he kissed her tenderly on the lips, "Sereena, are you okay, you are safe now."

She whispered, "I know you`d come."

They made their way out of the building to the palace with urgency Xavier met them, his eyes narrowed as he looked at Sereena, he had sense something off, her interaction with Balendin seamed unnatural, the connection wasn`t how it should be, it seemed empty, no emotions. Xavier has his suspicions that that wasn`t Sereena, but he was keeping it to himself for now, watching and observing, having a feeling that Icarus was up to something. This would not be the first time that he planted someone in the palace, as he recalls Aeneas, who took Aurelius.

Xavier looked across at Aurelius, who in turned was watching Xavier, he had picked up something wasn`t right and strolled over to Xavier, turned his back to the room as he spoke, "You are thinking, what am thinking?"

Xavier turned his head slightly to the side to engage with Aurelius, "Hmm, it depends on what you are thinking?"

Aurelius short heavy sigh, "That`s not Sereena."

Xavier felt his heart sink as he said the words, "No, it`s not, the interaction is fake."

"What, next?" Aurelius asked.

"We wait, we watch, there's a larger conspiracy at play." Xavier pointed out.

They both looked into the room as Balendin sat beside Sereena's bed holding her hand, Aurelius felt for his brother and know how he would feel if he found out.

Aurelius had a sinking feeling this wasn't over, this was the beginning of something a lot bigger, but he needed to return to his family on Earth.

Returning to New York, Aurelius knew that their journey was far from over.

Chapter 3

Aurelius safely returned to his time feeling a bit confused with all this time travelling, knowing he had to travel to the future to get to this home planet. The morning, to him first day back, to his timeline he only had a few days off, Catherine watched from the window, her heart swelling with pride and anxiety, "Be safe," she whispered, he fingers lightly touching the glass.

Arriving at the precinct, he was greeted by the familiar faces of his colleagues, "Chief, welcome back!" Officer Reynolds called out, a broad smile on his face.

"Thanks, Reynolds, it's good to be back," Aurelius replied, feeling mix of relief and apprehension.

The precinct was bustling with activity, Aurelius quickly immersed himself in the work he had missed, however, the weight of his experiences on Xyphoria Prime lingered in the back of his mind as he sat at his desk reviewing case files, his mind often drifted back to lush parks and cascading plants of his home planet, He wondered how long it would take for him to readjust to life on Earth.

Aurelius's know his morning was going to be full and the afternoon was going to be no different, meeting with his team to discuss an ongoing investigation. Detective Harris, his right-hand man, noticed the change in his demeanor, "Everything alright, Chief?" he asked with concern in his voice.

Aurelius nodded, though his thoughts were elsewhere, "Yeah, just getting back into the swing of things."

Meeting continued, Aurelius forced himself to focus, pushing aside the memories that tugged at his heart, he had a duty to uphold, and his team relied on his leadership as well as his family here on Earth and Xyphoria Prime.

The afternoon soon went to evening, Aurelius decided to call it the night, the day felt long and all he wanted to do was go home and be with his family, Catherine and Caius.

Days turned into weeks, Aurelius and Catherine found a new balance in their lives, work kept him busy, but he always had time for his family, finding joy in the smallest moments that made their life special.

Cathrine and Caius had decided to take a trip into the city, Aurelius thought this was a great opportunity to leave work early and meet them in Central Park. Walking through the city he had a deep sense of contentment, looking around the big city and finally reaching the park. He remembered it was one of Catherine's favourite places and having their fourth date here. Passing the large fountain, he felt a pang of longing, he hadn't thought about home for a while, Balendin came into his thoughts and wondered what Xavier had found out as heard nothing. As he turned the corner and saw Catherine and their son waiting for him, he realized that home wasn't a place, it was the people he loved.

Embracing his family, he could feel the love, he knows the journey wasn't over, but Catherin and Caius by his side, he was ready to face whatever the future held. They walked through the park and watched the sun set as it castes a warm glow over the city. Aurelius felt a renewed sense of purpose. He was Chief Martin Peters, a protector of the city, loving husband, and a devoted father, believing with family by his side, knowing he could overcome any challenge.

Life in New York was not without its difficulties, but it was also filled with love, laughter and endless possibilities, as they continue to build their future, Aurelius knew that no matter where their journey took them, they would always find their way back to each other.

With the weeks that followed were a whirlwind of activity, Aurelius found himself balancing the demands of his job with the needs of his family, what with the surge of crime, and his presence was needed more than ever. Despite all the chaos, he would find a quiet moment to reflect on his life, sitting at his desk, staring at the photo of his wife and child, thinking about the sacrifices they made and the strength they had shown. His heart swelled with pride and gratitude, they were his anchor, his reason for fighting every day.

His favourite time was being at home sharing stories about their day, Catherine taking about her work at the library and looking at her as her eyes lighting up as she recounted a particular interesting book or a conversation with a patron. Aurelius loved these moments, the way Catherine's passion for her work shone through, reminding him of why he had fallen in love with her. Sitting on the porch on long summers night, seeing the city lights twinkling as dusk falls, holding Catherine in his arms, a wave of emotions washing over him, seeing love in her eyes, the desire, stroking her neck as she lays her head on his chest, her soft skin as he moves slowly down her chest and lifting her chin as to steal a breathless kiss, but gazing into her eyes to see the desire in them, slowly stroke top of her breast and quickly pulling her closer passionately with one hand pulling her lips closer and other on the base of her back as she arched back, him guiding her on top of him, as her breath become deep and breathless , wanting her there and then. The passion was still there after all this time. For Catherine the tender moments, the connection, feeling safe in his arms, trusting him, needing him, showing him her pleasure as they go into ecstasy, sending her sensors heightened in a whirlwind. Their bond grew stronger, finding solace in each other's pleasure.

He still yet to tell her who he really is, everyday it eats him up, not able to tell her, the thought of keeping a secret from Catherine, hurts, her memories of him in the past was a man who did not know himself. Aurelius found himself often wondering what would happen if he did, how do you explain you are from another time and worse from another planet to an average person that would sound ridiculous. Fear was stopping him, fear of the consequences.

Aurelius took a deep breath, he desperately wanted to escape the hustle and bustle of the city as it takes its toll, longing to see the rolling mountains and lush green fields, wanting to feel a sense of peace, Aurelius felt a sense of peace he hadn't felt in a long time. Caius's laughter filled the car, and Catherine's smile was radiant. They spent the day exploring the countryside, hiking through forests and picnicking by a serene lake. Aurelius watched as Caius played, his heart swelling with joy. This was what life was about—these simple, precious moments. As the sun began to set, they sat by the lake, watching the colors dance across the water.

Aurelius pulled Catherine close, his voice soft. "I needed this. Being here with you and Caius, it's everything."

Catherine rested her head on his shoulder, her voice equally soft. "Me too. It's easy to get caught up in the chaos, but moments like this remind us of what's important."

Aurelius nodded, feeling a deep sense of gratitude. They had been through so much, but their love had only grown stronger. As they watched the sun dip below the horizon, Aurelius knew that no matter what challenges lay ahead, they would face them together. Back in the city, life returned to its usual pace. Aurelius was once again caught up in the whirlwind of work, but he carried the tranquillity of their countryside trip with him. It gave him a renewed sense of purpose, a reminder of why he did what he did.

Particularly challenging case brought Aurelius to the brink. The investigation was complex, and the stakes were high. As he poured over the case files late into the night, he felt a hand on his shoulder. He looked up to see Catherine, her eyes filled with concern.

"You're pushing yourself too hard," she said softly. "You need to rest."

Aurelius sighed, running a hand through his hair. "I know, but this case... it's important. I can't afford to miss anything."

Catherine knelt beside him; her voice gentle but firm. "You can't help anyone if you're burnt out. You need to take care of yourself too."

Aurelius looked into her eyes, feeling the weight of her words. She was right, as always. He needed to find a balance, for his sake and for his family.

He took a deep breath, nodding. "You're right. I'll finish up here and get some rest."

Catherine smiled, pressing a kiss to his forehead. "Good. We'll get through this together."

With her support, Aurelius found the strength to keep going. The case eventually ended, and the precinct celebrated their success. Aurelius felt a sense of accomplishment, but he knew that his true strength came from the love and support of his family.

As they settled into bed that night, Aurelius wrapped his arms around Catherine, his voice filled with emotion. "Thank you for always being my rock. I couldn't do this without you."

Catherine smiled; her eyes filled with love. "And I couldn't do this without you. We're a team, Martin, always."

Aurelius held her close, feeling a deep sense of contentment. Their journey was far from over, but with Catherine and Caius by his side, he knew they could face anything. Together, they would continue to build their future, one filled with love, laughter, and endless possibilities.

Chapter 4

The night was cold and silent as Aurelius walked through the streets of New York. His mind was a whirlwind of thoughts and emotions, reflecting the turmoil that had taken root in his heart. The recent events on Xyphoria Prime still haunted him, and he found himself questioning his choices more frequently than ever. As he approached his home, he stopped and looked up at the night sky, wondering if he had made the right decision to return to Earth.

Inside, Catherine was putting Caius to bed. She could sense the distance growing between them, a gap that neither of them seemed able to bridge. When Aurelius finally came through the door, she greeted him with a tired smile. "Long day?" she asked, trying to keep the worry out of her voice.

Aurelius nodded, his face etched with fatigue. "Yeah, it's been a tough one," he replied, avoiding her gaze.

As he settled into the couch, Catherine joined him, their shoulders barely touching. The silence between them was heavy, filled with unspoken fears and doubts. "You seem different, Martin/Aurelius," she finally said, breaking the tension. "What's been bothering you?"

Aurelius sighed, running a hand through his hair. "It's just... everything. The precinct, the cases, our time on Xyphoria Prime. I can't stop thinking about it."

Catherine placed a hand on his arm, her eyes filled with concern. "You don't have to carry this burden alone, you know. We're a team."

Aurelius felt a surge of guilt. He knew she was right, but he couldn't shake the feeling of isolation that had settled over him. "I know, Catherine. I just... I need some time to process everything."

She nodded, her heart aching for him. "Take all the time you need, Martin. I'll be here when you're ready to talk."

The days turned into weeks, and the distance between them grew. Aurelius threw himself into his work, using it as a distraction from the turmoil inside him. But no matter how hard he tried, the memories of Xyphoria Prime kept creeping back, haunting his every thought.

Aurelius was working late at the precinct; he received a call from Balendin. "Aurelius, I need your help," Balendin's voice was filled with desperation. "Sereena has been having nightmares ever since we returned. She's not herself."

Aurelius felt a pang of guilt. He had been so wrapped up in his own struggles that he hadn't been there for his friend. "I'm sorry to hear that, Balendin. I'll come as soon as I can."

He arrived at Balendin's apartment in the future New York, he was greeted by the sight of Sereena, pale and trembling, sitting on the couch. Balendin's face was etched with worry. "She's been like this for weeks," he said, his voice breaking. "I don't know what to do."

Aurelius knelt beside Sereena, his heart aching for her. "Sereena, can you tell me about your nightmares?"

She looked at him, her eyes filled with fear. "They're not just nightmares, Aurelius. They feel so real. I see Icarus, and he's... he's trying to take me back."

Aurelius felt a chill run down his spine. The trauma of their experiences was deeper than he had realized. "You're safe now, Sereena. Icarus can't hurt you anymore."

Sereena shook her head, tears streaming down her face. "But it feels so real. I can hear his voice, feel his touch. It's like he's still here."

Balendin wrapped his arms around her, his own eyes glistening with tears. "We'll get through this, Sereena. Together."

Aurelius felt a surge of determination. "We'll find a way to help you, Sereena. You're not alone in this."

As he left Balendin's apartment that night and travelled back to his timeline in Moden day New York, Aurelius felt a renewed sense of purpose. He needed to be there for his family, just as they had been there for him. And he needed to find a way to heal the wounds that still lingered.

As he entered home, he found Catherine waiting for him, her eyes filled with questions. "Is everything okay?" she asked, her voice trembling.

Aurelius took her hand, his heart heavy with the weight of his emotions. "No, Catherine. It's not. I've been so lost in my own struggles that I haven't been there for you or for our family. I need to do better."

Catherine pulled him into a tight embrace, her voice soothing. "We'll get through this, Martin. Together."

In the days that followed, Aurelius made a conscious effort to be more present, both at home and at work. He spent more time with Caius, playing with him and reading him bedtime stories. He talked with Catherine about his fears and doubts, finding comfort in her unwavering support.

He also reached out to his colleagues at the precinct, opening about his experiences on Xyphoria Prime, who are from there. To his surprise, they were more understanding and supportive than he had expected. Detective Harris became a confidant, offering a listening ear and sage advice.

One evening, as they were wrapping up a particularly challenging case, Detective Harris pulled Aurelius aside. "You've been through a lot, Chief. It's okay to lean on us when you need to."

Aurelius nodded, feeling a sense of relief. "Thanks, Harris. I appreciate it."

As the weeks turned into months, Aurelius began to find a new balance in his life. He still carried the weight of his experiences, but he no longer felt so alone. He had his family, his friends, and his colleagues, all standing by his side.

One night, as he sat on the porch with Catherine, watching the stars twinkle above them, he felt a sense of peace he hadn't felt in a long time. "Thank you for always being here for me," he said, his voice filled with emotion.

Catherine smiled, her eyes shining with love. "We're a team, Martin. Always."

Aurelius knew that their journey was far from over, but with Catherine and Caius by his side, he felt ready to face whatever the future held. Together, they would continue to build their future, one filled with love, laughter, and endless possibilities.

But the peace was short-lived. A distress call from Elysia shattered their newfound tranquillity. A rebellion had broken out, and the planet was in chaos. King Orion himself had sent the message, pleading for their help.

Aurelius felt a surge of urgency. "I need to go," he said, his voice resolute. "Balendin needs us."

Catherine's eyes filled with fear, but she nodded. "Okay, Martin."

His heart heavy with the weight of the mission ahead and transported to future New York, from there they boarded the spacecraft, Aurelius felt a mix of dread and determination. He knew the journey would be dangerous, but he also knew that they couldn't abandon Elysia in its time of need.

The journey to Elysia was tense, filled with anticipation and fear. As he approached the planet, he could see the signs of conflict from space. Fires burned across the landscape, and smoke billowed into the sky.

When they landed, they were greeted by King Orion, his face etched with worry. "Thank you for coming," he said, his voice filled with relief. "We need all the help we can get."

Aurelius felt a surge of determination. "We'll do whatever it takes to restore peace," he replied, his voice steady.

As they delved into the heart of the conflict, Aurelius found himself facing new challenges and old enemies. The rebellion was more complex and dangerous than they had anticipated, and the stakes were higher than ever.

Throughout the turmoil, Aurelius drew strength from his family. Thinking of Catherine's unwavering support and Caius's innocent courage gave him the determination to keep fighting. He also found solace in his brother, Balendin, their bond growing stronger as they faced the dangers together.

As they prepared for a critical mission, Aurelius pulled Balendin aside. "We need to end this rebellion, Balendin. For Sereena, for our families, for Elysia and Xyphoria Prime."

Balendin nodded, his eyes filled with determination. "We'll do it, Aurelius. Together."

The battle was fierce, and the stakes were higher than ever. Aurelius fought with everything he had, driven by the love for his family and the desire to protect the planet that had become a second home.

In the end, their efforts paid off. The rebellion was quashed, and peace was restored to Elysia for now. As they stood amidst the ruins of the final battlefield, Aurelius felt a deep sense of fulfilment. They had faced the darkness and emerged victorious.

Chapter 5

Returning to Earth, Aurelius felt a renewed sense of purpose. He knew that their journey was far from over, and know with Catherine and Caius by his side, he felt ready to face whatever the future held. Aurelius looked at his family with a heart full of gratitude.

The sun dipped below the horizon, painting the sky in hues of orange and pink, Aurelius joined Catherine as she rocked Caius asleep and sat beside her as the cool summer breeze gentle breezed through the porch. He turned a looked at Catherine, a serene looked graced her face, his heart swelled with love and pride, this was his family, his everything, yet the secrets he kept threatened to unravel the peace they had found, he was ready.

"Catherine," he began softly, his voice trembling slightly. "There's something I need to tell you."

Catherine looked up at him, her eyes filled with concern, she could see he was struggling with something, his looked worried, "What is it, Martin?"

Taking a deep breath, he felt the weight of his words pressing down on him, "I haven't been entirely honest with you about my past."

Catherine` brows furrowed, her heart missed a beat, she stopped rocking Caius, "What do you mean?"

Aurelius felt his heart pounding in his chest, he had rehearsed this conversation a thousand times in his mind, now that the moment had arrived, the words seemed to escape him,

"My name isn't Martin Peters," he finally said, "It's Aurelius Starhaven."

Catherine sat back in sofa her eye's widened in shock, but she remained silent, waiting for him to continue.

Taking her hand in to his, trying to draw strength from her touch, "I come from a place called Xyphoria Prime. My real mother, Aurelia was the Queen there, she was named after a planet called Aurelia, she was from the planet Galoria. I was brought here from the very people who sought to harm our family. But now, I feel it's time you know the truth."

Tears welled up in Catherine's eyes, she looked down at their son, then back at him, "Why did you not tell me before, you should have trusted me."

Aurelius's voice cracked with emotion, "I was afraid, Catherine, afraid of what you might think, afraid of losing you and our son. I can't keep this from you any longer, you deserve to know who I really am."

Catherine sat in silence for a moment, processing everything he had just revealed. Aurelius could see the conflict in her eyes as she looked at him, the love she had for him battling with the shock of his confession. Finally, she spoke, her voice barely a whisper, "I need some time to think."

Aurelius nodded, understanding the gravity of his revelation, "Take all the time you need, just know this I love you and I always will."

His heart ached, a part of him know he did the right thing by telling her, but the look on her face that he did not trust her enough to tell her sooner, made him ache inside.

The few days were a blur of tension and uncertainty, Aurelius found himself again grappling with a whirlwind of emotions. Deep inside was relieved that the truth was finally out, but he was also terrified of what the future might hold, He wished he could turn the clocks back and perhaps tell her everything when they first met. He wondered if Catherine accepts him for who he truly was? Or would the truth drive a wedge between them, tearing their family apart?

As the air cooled down in the evening sun Aurelius was playing in the garden with their son when Catherine approached him. Her expression was calm, but there was a determination in her eyes that gave him hope.

"I've been thinking about what you told me, "She began, "and I realized that it doesn't change how I feel about you. You are still the man I fell in love with, the father of our child. She draws a deep breath, "Your past doesn't define you."

Aurelius felt a wave of relief wash over him; he stood up and embraced her, holding her tightly, "Thank you, Catherine, you don't know how much that means to me."

She pulled slightly back, looking into his eyes, "But I do want to know more about your home, about Xyphoria Prime and I want to meet your family."

Aurelius smiled, a sense of hope blossoming in his heart, "I would love that, I promise I'll tell you everything and by the way, you have already had."

Catherine jaw dropped," I have? Who and when?"

Chuckling replied, "Balendin is my brother, Xander is our father, Xavier is our guardian and protector, and Sereena is Balendin's partner."

Catherine scoffed a little laugh escaping her lips, "Well, that explains everything."

Feeling a bit puzzled Aurelius looked at her, "What do you?"

Catherine smiled as she moved closure to his chest. "Just the way they were."

Aurelius chucked as he recalled the peculiar behaviors and tightly drew Catherine closer, "Yeah, they are a bit weird."

Holding each other, Aurelius realized that the future was still uncertain, for the first time in a long time, he felt a sense of peace, knowing deep down they would face whatever challenges come their way. With love and understanding, they would build a future where secrets had no place.

Aurelius took a deep breath, feeling nervous, he needed to share Catherine the other part of his story and wasn't sure how she would take it. As they sat on the porch in silence enjoying the gentle summer breeze gentle rustling the dry leaves around them as the sun set. Catherine turned her attention to Martin/Aurelius she could see something was troubling him.

As she held their son, her eyes fixed on Aurelius, a mix of curiosity and concern etched on her face.

"There's more you need to know," Aurelius began, his voice steady but tinged with emotion. "I was kidnapped as a child by a man who wasn't my father."

Catherine's eyes widened in shock, her grip tightening on their son. "Kidnapped? What do you mean?"

Aurelius sighed as he ran his hand through his hair. "The man I grew up calling my father, Simon Peters, wasn't my real father, nor is Sephen my brother. He took me from my home, from my mother Aurelia, and my real father and brother. He had his reasons, twisted as they were, but it tore my family apart. They came looking for me more than once."

Tears welled up in Catherine's eyes as she listened, "How did you find out?"

Aurelius, voice cracking with the weight of the memories, "It took years, for a long time, I believed the lies he told me."

Aurelius tried to fight the emotions, a tear rolled down his face as he continued, "Over the years as I grow, fragments of my past would appear in my dreams, I thought they were nightmare's especial the one where I was taken. At the time I did not know they were real until it was all explained. Now pieces of a life I had forgotten are slowly returning. When I met my real family again, everything feels into place."

Aurelius rolled up his shirt sleeved and revealed the tattoo on his right wrist, Catherine quickly moved her hand over her mouth as she gasped and then moved closer to see it properly.

As she looked, she up at him, she could see the pain in his eyes, reliving the painful memories that haunt him and his family, "What does it say?"

Aurelius looked at it and run his fingers over it. "It says Valens Incedo."

Puzzled Catherine stroked his wrist, "What does it mean?"

With a heavy sigh, Aurelius explained, "It means 'I go forward with courage, integrity, and every other positive quality,' it's in Latin a very old language."

Catherine reached out taking his hand in to hers, "Am so sorry Martin, I can't imagine what that must have been like for you. The tattoo proves who you truly are. Martin, sorry Aurelius, I love you no matter what your past holds."

Squeezing her hand to draw strength from her touch, he spoke, "I still cannot get used to that name, it feels strange but comforting, if that makes sense. To be honest, Catherine, it was hard, but it also led me to where I am today, with you and our son, Caius and for that I am grateful.

She nodded, hers full of understanding, "You've already met my family," he took a moment and continued, "Balendin is my brother, Sereena, as you know is his partner, Xander is my father and Xavier is my friend and guardian, they are not just my friends, there my real family.

As he just about to finished he remembered Isabell, "And Isabell knows."

Catherine's expression softened as she looked at him, "Thank you for telling me the truth, so Isabell knows?"

Aurelius started to chuckle as he stared into the street and replied, "Yes, she guessed."

Catherine smiled, "That doesn't surprise me, she knows a lot."

Aurelius felt a surge of relief and love, "There's one more thing," he said, a hint of excitement in his voice, "I want to show you my home, Xyphoria Prime, but it will mean traveling to the future first."

Catherine's expression changed to surprise and concern as she pulled herself up and looked at him, "What? Why do we have to travel to the future and how?"

Reaching down onto the coffee table and opened an app on the phone, "Through this, it's a special phone designed by the man who kidnapped me, so it blends in."

Catherine took the phone and examined it closely, Intrigued," Is this a real phone?"

Aurelius nodded, "Yes, but I only call the other phones as they are linked."

Aurelius could see that Catherine was still confused and needed a bit more convincing, "So, tell me again, why do we have to go to the future?"

He could not contain his laughter any more knowing this was going to take some time for Catherine to understand but also to lighten the mood, he replied, "That's where our spaceship is."

Catherine looked at him in total shock, "You're kidding, right? You're playing with me."

Shaking his head laughing. "Nope. You'll see."

Feeling he is playing with her, but his sincerity was clear.

Aurelius was left sating on the Porch as Catherine put their son to bed, staring out at the cityscape beyond, that had become so familiar. The noise, the lights, the constant movement, everything he once found comforting now felt suffocating. His mind drifted to Xyphoria Prime, the lush landscapes, the tranquility, and the sense of belonging he felt there. The thought of moving back had been gnawing at him for weeks, but the decision was far from simple.

Catherine emerged from the hallway; her eyes filled with concern as she joined him. "Martin, you've been so distant lately. What's on your mind?"

Aurelius sighed, rubbing his temples. "It's Xyphoria Prime. I can't stop thinking about it. I miss it more than I can explain."

Catherine placed a hand on his arm, her touch grounding him. "Martin. If It felt like home rather that Earth never has. But what are you thinking? What's really bothering you?"

He turned to look at her, his eyes searching hers for understanding. "I've been thinking about moving back. Permanently. But it's more than just that. I've been considering resetting the timeline here on Earth, making it as if we never lived here."

Catherine's eyes widened in surprise. "Resetting the timeline? What do you mean?"

Aurelius took a deep breath, his voice trembling slightly. "As Keepers of Time we have the ability to alter the timeline, to erase our existence here. It would be like we never lived on Earth. No one would remember us; it would be as if we never existed in this timeline."

Catherine stared at him, a mix of emotions playing across her face. "That's a huge decision, Martin. We'd be leaving everything behind. Our friends, our life here, everything."

"I know," Aurelius replied, his voice heavy with emotion. "But think about it, Catherine. We could be happier on Xyphoria Prime. Caius will be happier. We could start fresh, without the burdens and memories that haunt us here and Caius is young enough to adapt."

Catherine sat silently for a moment, her mind racing. She would love their life on Xyphoria Prime, the peace, the beauty, the simplicity. But the idea of erasing their existence on Earth was daunting. "Okay, but what about our friends and colleagues here? What about the lives we've touched?"

Aurelius tried to mentally prepare Catherine what to expect as they prepared for their journey to Xyphoria Prime, but she needed to experience herself and not through his eyes. With everything in place and Isabell knowing where they are, Aurelius took out his other phone and pressed the app and everything went round in circles, He was getting use to the time travel as had done it a few times and not been sick.

Catherine looked around in absolute astonishment, "You weren't kidding."

He chuckled in amusement. He loved the way Catherine is seeing a whole different life, "Nope, but this is only the beginning of the journey. We will look around when we return."

Aurelius approach the spot where Balendin had hid the space craft and returned in another in what was Central Park, now a thick forest, it instantly recognized him and appeared when he got closer.

Catherine's jaw dropped as she saw the craft reveal itself, "How does it know?"

Aurelius wasn't sure if he should say the long verse or the short," Its due to our DNA and the craft scans me as I approach."

Catherine run her hand across the sleek, smooth, elongated oval body in bewilderment. The craft had soft, ambient lighting running along the edges which provided visibility and aesthetic appeal.

Catherine looked at emblem on the side and asked, "Is this Xyphoria Prime's emblem?"

Aurelius smiled and nodded and began to explain what it all means. About the Phoenix being, Rebirth, renewal, time, eternity, legacy, continuity, the control over time, balance of life cycles. He also went on to explain that Phoenix holding a small clock means rebirth, renewal and immortality rising from the ashes, represents time, combined, signify the eternal nature of time and the cyclical process of renewal and transformation. Xyphoria Prime recognizes the importance of time in growth and the continuous process of improvement and evolution.

She still could not believe that she had a space craft in front of her, it was huge, "How long will it take us to reach Xyphoria Prime?"

Aurelius thought about, "Technically five years at WOP speed one thousand times the speed of light, but in this one year."

Catherine's gasped, it had just blown her mind, "What do you mean five years?

"I do it all the time and go back the day I left, that's why we are the Keepers of Time."

This was too much, she had no idea, the magnitude of all this, but Martin/Aurelius tried to explain further, but it was hard to put into words.

With heart racing, Catherine for a minute thought they had done this, "Okay, so have we done this before?"

Shaking his head, "No, we haven`t." Her next question was, "So, when you return to the time you left, what happens to the timeline on Xyphoria?"

"Nothing, it stays the same, it`s a different timeline." Martin/Aurelius tried to reassure her, but know she needed to see for herself to understand."

They entered the craft, Catherine and Caius wondered round the craft taking in its vastness, the living quarters were designed for long voyages, they were spacious and equipped with all necessary amenities. The walls are adorned with dynamic panels that can display any chosen environment or scenery, creating a comfortable and customization atmosphere. The quarters also included sleeping pods, a common lounge area, and a dinning section with a food synthesizer that can create meals from raw molecular ingredients. It even had a recreation facility, including a virtual reality chamber for entertainment and training simulations. The spacecraft had everything they ever needed and so much more.

As they wondered around marveling at everything, Catherine and Caius eventually found Aurelius at the control center which was located at the front with panoramic view that provides by a transparent, nearly indestructible canopy.

As they stood there Catherine mouth dropped as she could see the trees, the sky everything and did not know where to look. Aurelius looked across at Catherine smiling, "Wait until we are in space, even more spectacular."

He settled in seating area the seats which were made of a memory material that adapts to occupant`s body for comfort as the craft goes into hyper drive. Catherine sat next to him there was so much she did not understand but wanted to. Martin/Aurelius rested his hand on her lap and squeezed her knee as he knows what she was thinking reassuring her in time she will.

Sitting back in the comfy seats Martin/Aurelius command the craft to take off, all the controls light up came to life and holographic popped up above the panels that looked like a map of the universe.

Catherine gasped, "Won`t people see us?"

Chuckling Aurelius answered, "No, its energy shield has been activated, its invisible to the naked eye, the shield will shimmer with a faint blue hue."

"What about the noise?"

Aurelius started laughing, her innocence, was endearing, "Relax, stop worrying, Catherine, it is silent and not only that if they do, but they will also think it's the wind and besides this is the future and they have flying cars."

The craft gently raised above the trees, the city into the atmosphere, it went from light to dark. Caius looked in wonder and pointing excitable at the stars. Wanting to know what they were and if anyone lived there, for a four-year-old his mind was inquisitive. The craft went into hyper-drive, and everything went zooming past as they went through different galaxies.

Aurelius couldn`t wait to show Catherine and Caius the place that he had once called home or is it still home?

Earth is what he knows and the life with Catherine, but a part of him was torn between the two worlds and timeline. Xyphoria Prime in the Andromeda Galaxy which was one of the closest galaxies to the Milky Way, positioned in a relatively peaceful sector known for its rich star clusters and vibrant nebulae which benefits from a stable environment that supports its diverse ecosystem and advance civilization. The air on the planet is clear and no pollution, animals ranging from domestic cats and dogs which some took from Earth for pets to the exotic, with little pockets of parks, fountains, forest with hidden secret groves, mountains and waterfalls. The most important thing on Xyphoria Prime was the fact that the atmosphere was rejuvenating and the water, that promote better cellular regeneration. These Bioluminescent particles float in the atmosphere, emitting soft healing glow, rich in vitamins and antioxidants that absorb through the skin and respiratory system aiding cellular repair. The air also contains a slight ionized its maintained by the planet's unique electromagnetic field and naturally occurring plasma storms. That they don't get old, they were an envy of some planets...

Aurelius explained their diet, what they eat and that they have a fascinating diet that influenced by the planet's diverse ecosystem. The fruits on the planet were even more exotic, glowfruit which grows on tree and emit a gentle glow, rich in nutrients with a sweet, tangy flavor which they harvest and trade with other planets. The crystal kelp found in the crystal-clear oceans of Xyphoria Prime, this kelp is prized with its crunchy texture and mineral content. The rock worms were delicacy, Aurelius did not care for this even though it was protein rich, Catherine pulled a face where Caius laughed at the prospect of eating worms and said he would. There was some many question they both had, they only simply way for Martin/Aurelius to explain and for them to experience for their self's.

The Journey was smooth they didn't notice what speed the craft was doing over 2000 WAP drive. Caius had fallen asleep in one of the pods along with Catherine and was missing the best parts of the journey, Aurelius had already let his family know they were coming, and all was in place for their arrival. Catherine had only packed toothbrushes as everything was provided, except for Martin/Aurelius as he insisted taking his Earth clothes with him as did not feel comfortable in theirs.

The craft started to slow down as it approached the Andromeda galaxy it would be another two hours before they arrive to the planet, Martin/Aurelius decided to get some sleep in the pods in the quarters where Catherine and Caius were.

Two hours had flown by, the computer woke Aurelius that they would be arriving in five minutes.

He gently woke his family, still dazed Catherine spoke, "Are we here?

Aurelius nodded as he prepared his family to leave the craft, as they landed the doors opened and standing there was Xander and Balendin waiting patiently as they excited the craft.

Balendin was the first to welcome his brother, "Welcome home Aurelius."

Xander stepped forward and hugged his son, "Good to see you, son."

Caius run forward into Xander's arms who instantly picked him up, "Are you, my granddad?"

Xander smiling nodded, "Yes, I am your Eldoren."

Aurelius wrapped his arm round Catherine and pulled her close as he felt a sense of pride watching his father with his son. As they walked towards the craft lifted and left, Aurelius explained that it's gone in simple terms the garage. As they left the rooftop Catherine could see across the city and how high they were and gasp at the tall building and flying ships, the two moons, Aurelius reassured her they will see everything later once they settle in and had dinner, he tells her mind was working overtime as she gasped in awe.

Balendin guided them to the main dining room, the walls were deep, rich maroon or forest green, with white trim and gold accents, large mirrors, pot plants, chandeliers, Catherine looked at Aurelius and informed him it looks like modern, Aurelius laughed and explained that some of it did come from Earth, but the future Earth was some of their technology except the Tesla, there humans invention, Catherine looked across the room and saw two large floor to ceiling windows that adore the room letting the natural light shine through revealing the beautiful walls and the city itself. Lunch was spread on a lavish table with plush upholstered chairs in neutral tones light.

Caius was the first to sit pointing at the different foods that were on the table and a face of disappointment that there were no worms, everyone laughed at his disappointment, Xander reassured him he will have some for dinner. Their lunch was light with skyberries tart for dessert, for the main luminfish delicate steamed, bread made from spiral grain, veilshroom with crystal kelp that grow in the ocean. It all looked delicious, Sereena came halfway through and apologized for being late as she turned her attention to kiss Balendin as she had pressing things to deal with first.

Aurelius took Catherine's hand as they finished lunch and walked her through the vastness of the palace. The hallway featured a sophisticated combination of matte navy-blue lower walls with white wainscoting, transitioning to a lighter. The top half was an airy blue, crystal chandeliers interspersed, on the walls were panels, Catherine asked inquisitively what they were for, Aurelius raised his arm and flashed it in front of the screen, the lights turned on, she stood with mouth wide open in amazement. Aurelius watched her reaction in awa, his heart was joyful that Catherine had wanted to come here and see what he sees.

Grabbing her hand, "There's more to see, but first you need to change your clothes."

She could not take her eyes of ceiling and in astonishment replied, "There's more, you've got to be kidding me!"

Aurelius laughed and then realization kicked in as the words left his mouth, "Yes, you'll like the clothes, after all you are married to a Prince."

Catherine took her eyes of the ceiling and stopped and gently pulled him back towards her at looked at him with a confused expression, "I am?"

Aurelius felt strange inside at the realization of who he really is as it sank in, "Yes, I can't get use to that or my real name, but now you're here I can."

Still trying to comprehend what Aurelius had just said, "So, Xander your father is the King?"

Aurelius nodded, "Yes, Balendin is a Prince and Sereena is a princess from Elysia, Xavier is from Elaria, soon you will meet my sister Rebecca/Stella."

Catherine let go of Aurelius hand and sat on one of the many lavish sofas along the hallway that directly faces the large windows looking out on to the city as she tried to process, sister echoed in her head, he had never mentioned her before.

Taking a deep breath Catherine whispered, "You have a sister?"

Aurelius moved forward and knelt beside here and placed his hand on her knee and other hand on her shoulders, seeing on her face this was a lot of formation," Catherine, you, okay?"

Wiping a tear from her face she whispered. "You never mentioned her before, until now."

Aurelius pulled himself up and sat next to Catherine taking her hand into his, "Am sorry, I should have mentioned her before, she is hardly here as always traveling to Aurelia planet with her fiancé Prince Elion Verdant."

Catherine was overwhelmed and tied; Aurelius could see that. "Tell you what, let's go and lay down and in the evening, we go and look at the city, it's even more spectacular."

Catherine nodded in acceptance hand in hand they walked towards the hidden lift rather than take the stairs. As they stepped inside Catherine marveled at the interior running her hand across the sleek lift that re-flexed the advanced technology of Xyphoria Prime along with transparent walls, with stunning views, Aurelius did not care to look as still felt uncomfortable with heights.

Aurelius walked into to their bedroom the room was even grander, warm muted tones like taupe, luxurious fabric wall panels behind the bed the other wall featured a sophisticated, a large-scale geometric pattern in metallic hues. The furniture was custom made in dark wood with elegant upholstery headboard.

Catherine looked at the size of the bed, "Wow, that's huge, am going get lost in that."

Aurelius chucked as he undressed and climbed into bed, with a cheeky grin taped the covers, "Come to bed, Catherine."

Smiling, walked slowly to the bed teasing him as she moved towards him Aurelius waited patiently, watching as she removed each item seductively, as she reached his side of the bed she removed the last item, Aurelius pulled the covers and gently took her hands and guided her on top of him. Their needs were obvious, sensual and deep, they made love, their love for one another was deep.

It was six hours until Aurelius and Catherine arose from bed feeling rejuvenated after their sleep, came down for dinner, they enter the dining room. the room full of chatter and Caius in full swing enjoying himself with his Uncle's, Auntie Sereena and Eldoren, his grandfather, laughing and joking.

Aurelius and Catherine stood by the door watching, their hearts filled with joy, Aurelius turned to Catherine, "This is our family, soon it will be complete with my sister Stella."

Wiping a tear from her cheek she know exactly what Aurelius was talking about, her parents had died some time ago and Caius did not get to meet them, but he always enjoyed playing with Xander and Balendin whenever they came to visit, the house was always filled with laughter., now even more so. Aurelius was right this is our family, and it will be completed when Stella returns.

Time seamed to go fast by the time dinner had finished and everyone left the table, taking Catherine's hand Aurelius guided her up and walked out of the palace to show her the city in all its glory. Catherine gasped in awe as she saw the tall building reaching towards the sky with some plants cascading down the sides, greenery blundering seamless with sleek architecture. Xyphoria Prime was breathtaking with parks dotted in the city, trees and small tranquil water fountains adding soothing ambiance to the bustling environment.

Aurelius pointed out various landmarks, sharing some of his childhood that he remembered, gesturing to a park with vibrant flowers, "This is where I used to play as a child."

Catherine could see in his expressions he was masking his sadness but, on few occasions, caught a glimpse of the sadness in his eyes. It broke her heart to see it, she could not imagine what he must be going through as the memories returned and the anger he must have been feeling. Catherine listened intently, her eyes widened with wonder, she could see the love Aurelius had and the sorrow as he talked about his mother. Her heart swelling with happiness.

Squeezing his hand as they take a gentle stroll through the park looking around her, she whispered, "It's beautiful, thanking you for bringing me here."

Aurelius smiled, feeling a deep sense of contentment, "Am so glad you're here with me, there's more I want to show you."

Catherine felt a sense of belonging she hadn't expected, spending a few days exploring the city, meeting his family and feeling like home and understood why this place meant so much to Aurelius.

As the evening drawn in Catherine and Aurelius sat by a fountain, Aurelius turn to Catherine, his eyes fille with emotion, "I was afraid to tell you the truth, to show you this part of my life,"

Aurelius took a deep breath as he tried to find words to express how he is feeling, "Seeing you here, I know I made the right decision. I love you, Catherine, and I want to build a future with you, no secrets, no lies."

Catherine's eyes shimmered with tears, and she learned in to kiss him, "I love you too, Martin," with a wink, "Sorry Aurelius, am ready to face whatever the future holds, as long as we are together."

The sun set over Xyphoria Prime, painting the sky with hues of orange and pink, Aurelius felt a sense of peace he hadn't known in years. With Catherine by his side, he knew they could overcome challenges. Together, they would create a future filled with love, truth, and endless possibilities.

The days turned into weeks on Xyphoria Prime, Aurelius, and their son settled into a comfortable routine. Catherine found herself captivated by the planet's serene beauty and advanced technology. The blend of nature and futuristic architecture fascinated her, and she often spent hours exploring the city with their son, marvelling at the wonders around them.

One afternoon, as Aurelius visited an old friend, Catherine took their son Caius to a nearby park. She watched as he played with other children, his laughter echoing through the air. A smile spread across her face, but her mind wandered back to their life on Earth. She missed the familiarity of New York, the hustle and bustle of the city that never slept.

As the sun began to set, casting a golden glow over the park, Aurelius arrived, his expression thoughtful, taking her hand as he sat next to her on the bench, "Catherine, there's something we need to discuss,"

She looked at him, concern etching her features, "What is it Martin... Aurelius?"

Taking a deep breath, his eyes reflecting the warmth of the setting sun, "It's time we returned to our own time."

Catherine nodded, understanding the weight of his words with a heavy heart, "I know, as much as I love this planet, our life is there.

Caius ran up to them, his face flushed with excitement, "Daddy, are we going back home?"

Aurelius lifted him into his arms, smiling, "Yes, little man, we'll going back soon."

Aurelius reflected on his journey, the revelation of his identity had brought a whirlwind of emotions, but it had also brought a sense of clarity. He was no longer living in the shadows of his past; he was embracing his future with Catherine and Caius by his side.

The journey back to Earth was filled with a mix of anticipation and nostalgia. Aurelius couldn't help but think about the moment this family founds him on Earth. The pain in his father Xander's eyes, the determination in Balendin's voice as they revealed the truth to him, and the overwhelming sense of belonging that had washed over him when he was reunited with them.

Aurelius started to have flashbacks he remembered years ago, on Earth, Aurelius had been living as Martin Peters, unaware of his true heritage, while walking through Central Park, he noticed a group of people watching him intently. Among them was a man with a commanding presence and a look of profound sorrow in his eyes, it was Xander, his real father.

"Martin," the man called out, his voice thick with emotions, "Or should I say, Aurelius."

Aurelius froze, his heart racing, "Who are you? How do you know my name and who is Aurelius?"

Fighting back the tears, Xander whispered, "Am sorry my son... His voice breaking as he trying to control his emotions, "I'm your father," gesturing to the right Xander introduced Balendin as his brother.

Balendin, his eyes filled with mix of relief and determination, he wanted so much to make this process easy, "We've been searching for you for years, Aurelius." He stopped mid-sentence searching for any recognized in Aurelius's face.

Aurelius felt a rush of memories flood his mind, fragments of a life he had forgotten, the realization hit him like a tidal wave, and he stumbled back, struggling to process the truth.

His voice trembled with emotion, "Why did you wait so long to find me?"

Tears streaming down his face, Xander replied "We never stopped searching." Xander bowed his head, "It wasn't until; recently that we found a clue leading us to you here."

Balendin placed a reassuring hand on his brother's shoulder, "We know this a lot to take in, but we want to help you remember who you are." Balendin could feel his emotions rising, swollen hard, "Come back with us to Xyphoria Prime.

Aurelius nodded, overwhelmed but determined to uncover the truth, he confronted the man who had taken him from his family, then everything went dark, and all had been forgotten as if his memory had been wiped clean.

The journey that followed was filled with moments of revelation and reunion after the man who took him, died, they had to try to reconnect with him in a different way, but along that journey he had meet Sereena, Xavier and Rebecca/Stella each one filling in the missing pieces of his past. The tattoo on his wrist, a symbol of his heritage, was a constant reminder of his identity.

The ship approached future Earth, Aurelius turned to Catherine, who had been quietly reflecting on her time on Xyphoria Prime.

Turning to Catherine place his hand on her`s, his voice gentle, "Are you ready?"

Catherine smiled, her eyes filled with love, hiding her thoughts, "Yes, let`s go home."

Pulling Catherine closer he gazed into her eyes, her hand gently touching his chest as his hand touched her neck softly, she let out a gasp as she felt his touch gently caressing, he leaned in stealing a kiss, whispering, "This moment in time is where I want to be.... with you and Caius." His heart felt at peace, family meant everything to him.

Reaching the city as the sun went down, the moon made appearance, shining against the dusky sky, the stars were just about to make show as the sun disappeared over the horizon. Aurelius stopped, taking Catherine`s hand pulling her close, his heart had a sense of gratitude they both had taken. Looking her eyes he thought about the journey he had taken, never believing the course of action would bring Catherine and his child back, she and Caius was his life, he`s every being, wanting his family back...to protect the future. He reached into his pocket and took his phone out, pressed the appt transporting his family back to their time. They had been away a long time, but Aurelius had reset the time zone to two weeks after their left so not to arouse suspicion.

Aurelius sat alone in the quiet of the night, reflecting on the journey that had brought him here. His thoughts drifted to his mother, Aurelia, and the life he had left behind. The weight of his responsibilities as both a father and a hidden prince bore heavily on his shoulders. Yet, in Catherine's acceptance, he found a renewed strength. She was his anchor, and her love was beacon of hope in the uncertainty of their path ahead.

Catherine too, was deep in thought, she had sensed there was more to him than he let on, but the truth was beyond her wildest imagination. The revelation of his royal lineage and the existence of Xyphoria Prime had shaken her, but it had also opened her eyes to the depth of his sacrifices and the love he had for her and their son. As she laid in bed, she felt a mixture of fear and excitement for the future, but was determined to stand by his side, no matter what challenges lay ahead.

Aurelius looked down, his heart aching. "It's not an easy decision. But I can't shake the feeling that Xyphoria Prime is where we belong. Where Caius can grow up safe and happy. Where we can be truly free."

Catherine took his hand, her eyes filled with love and understanding. "If it's what you truly want, Martin, then I'll support you. I love Xyphoria Prime too. I felt a connection there that I've never felt anywhere else. And if it means being together as a family, then I'm willing to make that sacrifice."

Aurelius felt a surge of relief and gratitude. "Thank you, Catherine. Your support means everything to me."

They spent the next few days in deep discussion, weighing the pros and cons, talking about the future, and what it would mean for Caius. The decision was not made lightly, but with each passing day, they grew more certain that moving to Xyphoria Prime was the right choice.

One evening, as they sat together on the couch, Martin/Aurelius took Catherine's hand. "We need to talk to Caius about this. He deserves to know what's happening and to have a say in our decision."

Catherine nodded, her heart aching at the thought of the conversation. "You're right. He's a smart boy. He'll understand."

They called Caius into the living room, and Aurelius knelt down to his level. "Caius, your mom and I have been talking about something very important. How would you feel about moving to Xyphoria Prime? Permanently."

Caius's eyes lit up with excitement. "Really? We can go back. I loved it there!"

Aurelius smiled, his heart swelling with love for his son. "Yes, we can. But it means we might not see our friends here on Earth again. It would be a big change."

Caius thought for a moment, then nodded decisively. "I want to go. Xyphoria Prime is the best place ever!"

Catherine hugged Caius tightly, tears streaming down her face. "Alright, then. We'll go."

The decision made; they began the process of preparing for the move. Martin/Aurelius reached out to Balendin and the other allies they had made on Xyphoria Prime, ensuring that their

transition would be smooth. They also began the complex task of resetting the timeline on Earth.

Aurelius consulted with Xavier, whose abilities as a medium were crucial in executing the timeline reset. "Are you sure about this, Aurelius?" he asked, his eyes filled with concern.

Aurelius nodded, determination in his eyes. "Yes, Xavier. We're sure. This is what's best for our family."

Xavier sighed, then began the intricate process. The room filled with a soft, ethereal light as he chanted ancient words, his hands moving gracefully through the air. Aurelius held Catherine and Caius close, feeling a mix of fear and hope.

As the ritual reached its climax, a wave of energy washed over them, and the world around them seemed to shimmer and blur. When the light finally faded, they found themselves standing on the familiar soil of Xyphoria Prime.

Aurelius looked around, his heart pounding. They were back, but more importantly, they were together. "We did it," he whispered, tears streaming down his face.

Catherine smiled; her eyes filled with tears of joy. "We did. We're home."

Caius ran ahead, laughing and exploring the beautiful surroundings. Martin/Aurelius watched him, feeling a deep sense of peace and fulfillment. They had made the right choice. This was where they belonged.

Over the next few weeks, they settled into their new life on Xyphoria Prime. They lived in the palace with their own wing. Martin/Aurelius found a new purpose, working to protect and serve the people of Xyphoria Prime, while Catherine immersed herself in the community, finding ways to contribute and make a difference.

As evening approach, they sat by a tranquil lake, watching the twin moons rise, Martin/Aurelius took Catherine's hand. "Thank you for believing in me, for trusting me. This is the life I always dreamed of, but I never thought it was possible."

Catherine smiled, leaning her head on his shoulder. "We made it possible, together. And this is just the beginning."

As they watched the stars twinkle in the night sky, Martin/Aurelius felt a deep sense of contentment. They had faced countless challenges, but their love had carried them through. And as they looked to the future, they knew that no matter what lay ahead, they would face it together, on the planet that had become their true home.

The peace and beauty of Xyphoria Prime provided a perfect backdrop for their new life. Aurelius and Catherine found themselves growing closer than ever, their bond strengthened by the trials they had overcome. Taking long walks through the lush forests, explored hidden waterfalls, and spending quiet evenings under the stars, sharing their hopes and dreams for the future.

Caius thrived in his new environment, making friends and discovering a world full of wonder and adventure. Aurelius watched his son with pride, knowing that they had made the right choice for him. The freedom and beauty of Xyphoria Prime offered a life that Earth never could.

The sun set over the horizon, painting the sky with brilliant hues of orange and pink, Aurelius felt a sense of peace wash over him. This was where he was meant to be. This was home.

Catherine her face glowing with happiness. Aurelius entered, wrapping his arms around her from behind. "I missed you," he whispered, kissing her neck.

Catherine smiled, leaning into his embrace. "I missed you too. How was your day?"

"It was good, come we are gathering for dinner," Martin/Aurelius replied, his voice filled with contentment.

They gathered in the big dining room with Xander, Balendin, Sereena and Xavier sharing stories and laughter, their hearts full of gratitude for the life they had built. As the evening turned to night, they tucked Caius into bed, his face peaceful and content.

Aurelius and Catherine stood by the window, looking out at the starry sky. "We did the right thing," Aurelius said softly, his voice filled with conviction. "This is where we belong."

Catherine nodded, her heart swelling with love for her husband. "Yes, Martin. This is our home, and we're exactly where we're meant to be."

As they stood there, wrapped in each other's arms, Martin/Aurelius knew that their journey was far from over. But with Catherine and Caius by his side, he felt ready to face whatever challenges lay ahead. Together, they would continue to build a future filled with love, laughter, and endless possibilities, on the planet that had become their true home. As they enjoyed their tranquil life unto know to them there was something dark and sinister larking in the horizon, that was just about to be turned upside once again.

Chapter 6

Aurelius awoke startled he could hear people screaming, the palace hallways filled with chaos, quickly got dress and woke Catherine and Caius rushed out the door to their room and headed to the throne room were Balendin, Xander, Sereena, Xavier and the guards.

Aurelius flushed trying to catch his breath as he entered, "What's going on?"

Xander took a deep breath, his voice waved anxiety as he spoke, "We are under attack, Icarus has sent his army, we need to act quick."

Aurelius stepped outside and looked up he gasped as he saw the skies above Xyphoria Prime grew darker by the hour, a thick blanket of foreboding clouds swirling ominously. The air was charged with tension, the kind that made the hair on the back of your neck stand on end. Aurelius, Catherine, and their son stood together, watching the horizon with a mixture of dread and determination. Suddenly, a voice boomed across the landscape, echoing through the city like a clap of thunder, the ground shaking. It was a voice that seemed to come from the very depths of the darkness itself, malevolent and filled with rage. "Release Liber or face the annihilation of your world!"

Aurelius felt his blood run cold. The name Liber was like a curse, bringing back memories of pain. "They want Liber," he whispered, his voice tight with fear and anger.

Xander, standing beside him, clenched his fists. "We can't release him. The destruction he caused... it would be catastrophic."

The city erupted into chaos. Citizens ran through the streets, their faces twisted in fear as the voice echoed again. "Release him or watch your world burn!"

Aurelius turned to Xavier, who was already preparing his magic. Xavier's face was set with grim determination, his hands glowing with a bright, blue light. "I'll do what I can to keep the darkness at bay," Xavier said, his voice steady despite the chaos around them.

Xander closed his eyes, her brow furrowing in concentration. "We need to stay together. Our unity is our strength."

The streets of Xyphoria Prime were filled with panic. People screamed, tripping over one another in their desperate attempts to find safety. Aurelius's heart ached as he watched families huddling together, their faces pale with terror.

"We need to organize an evacuation," Catherine said, her voice firm. "Get the people to safety."

Aurelius nodded, his mind racing, "Father, gather our forces. Leo helped coordinate they people to safety. We need to move quickly."

As they moved to put their plan into action, the ground beneath them shook, a deep rumble that seemed to come from the very core of the planet. Aurelius's heart pounded in his chest. He knew they were running out of time and if they do not stop this the whole timeline will collapse as well as their world.

Xavier stood at the center of the city, his hands raised as he chanted in a language only, he and the ancient guardians of Xyphoria Prime could understand. A barrier of light began to form, pushing back the encroaching darkness. But Aurelius could see the strain on Xavier's face, the sweat trickling down his temples. It was clear that the effort was taking a toll.

"Xavier, are you alright?" Aurelius called out; his voice filled with concern.

Xavier nodded, but his eyes betrayed his exhaustion. "I can hold it for now, but we need a plan. This darkness is relentless."

Leo's eyes snapped open, a look of horror on his face. "It's not just the darkness. Something is coming from Zamathia Vortex. Something worse."

Aurelius's blood ran cold. He turned to Xander. "We need to find a way to stop this. We can't let them release Liber."

As they strategist, the darkness pressed harder against Xavier's barrier, the malevolent force testing their defenses. The air grew colder, and an unnatural silence fell over the city, broken only by the distant cries of terrified citizens.

Catherine held their son tightly, her eyes filled with worry. "Aurelius, we can't let anything happen to him."

"I won't," Aurelius said, his voice filled with determination. "We'll find a way to stop this."

The ground shook again, more violently this time, causing buildings to sway and cracks to form in the streets. Martin/Aurelius knew they were running out of time. "We need to confront whatever is coming from Zamathia Vortex," he said, his voice resolute.

Xavier took a stepped forward, his face pale but determined. "I can sense where it's coming from. We need to go to the source."

Aurelius, Xander, Xavier, and Leo gathered their forces, preparing to face the darkness head-on. Catherine insisted on coming with them, her eyes blazing with determination. "We're in this together," she said, her voice firm and handed Caius to Sereena who had emerged from inside the palace.

As they made their way towards the origin of the malevolent force, the atmosphere grew heavier, the air thick with an oppressive energy.

The sky above Zamathia Vortex was a swirling vortex of dark clouds, lightning flashing within them.

Aurelius's heart pounded in his chest as they approached a massive structure, the source of the dark energy. "This is it," Xavier said, his voice barely a whisper. "This is where we'll find our answers."

Inside the structure, the air was even colder, and the darkness seemed to pulse with a life of its own. Martin/Aurelius could feel the malevolent presence pressing in on them, threatening to overwhelm their senses.

"We need to stay strong," Xavier said, his voice steady. "Remember why we're here."

As they ventured deeper, they encountered resistance. Dark figures emerged from the shadows, their eyes glowing with a sinister light. Martin/Aurelius and Xander fought them off, their movements quick and precise. Xavier's abilities proved invaluable, guiding them through the maze-like corridors.

At the heart of the structure, they found a massive chamber. In the center stood an altar, surrounded by dark energy. And there, bound by chains of light, was a figure Martin/Aurelius recognized immediately—Liber.

"Release me," Liber demanded, his voice a low growl. "Or watch your world fall."

Aurelius's heart raced. He knew they couldn't release Liber, but the darkness pressing in around them left them with few options. "We need to destroy this place and close this portal," he said, his voice filled with determination.

Xavier nodded, his hands glowing with magical energy. "I can create a spell to collapse the structure, but it will take time."

Leo placed a hand on Xavier's shoulder. "I'll help. We can do this together."

As they began their work, the dark energy around them intensified. The ground shook violently, Aurelius could feel the oppressive force closing in on them. "We need to hold them off," he said, turning to Xander and Catherine. "Protect Xavier and Leo."

The battle was fierce, the dark figures relentless in their attack. But Aurelius, Xander, and Catherine fought with a determination born of desperation. They knew what was at stake, and they refused to back down.

Finally, Xavier and Leo completed the spell. The structure began to collapse, the dark energy dissipating as the walls crumbled around them. Aurelius grabbed Catherine's hand, pulling her towards the exit. "We need to get out, now!"

As they raced to safety, the ground continued to shake, the entire structure collapsing in on itself. They emerged into the open air just as the final walls fell, the dark energy dissipating into nothingness.

Aurelius turned to Xavier and Leo, a look of relief and gratitude on his face. "You did it. We did it."

Xavier nodded, his face pale with exhaustion. "The darkness is gone, for now. But we need to remain vigilant as it will return, Icarus does not give up that easily."

Aurelius looked at his family, their faces filled with relief and determination. "We'll protect our home, no matter what. Together, we're unstoppable."

As they made their way back to the city, the skies began to clear, the oppressive darkness lifting. The citizens of Xyphoria Prime emerged from their hiding places, their faces filled with hope.

Aurelius felt a deep sense of satisfaction. They had faced the darkness and emerged victorious. But he knew their journey was far from over as felt they will be back.

Turning to Catherine with concern, "Where's Caius?"

Catherine felt a pain in her pit of her stomach, "Sereena has him."

Aurelius quickly looked at the others as his heart felt a pain that cut deep and thought history repeating itself.

The skies over Xyphoria Prime were deceptively calm, a stark contrast to the turmoil that gripped Aurelius as he raced through the city streets. His heart pounded in his chest, his breath coming in ragged gasps. He couldn't shake the image in his head of Sereena's cold, determined eyes as she had taken their son, Caius. The betrayal cut deep, a wound that seemed to bleed with every step he took.

Aurelius's mind raced, a thousand thoughts colliding. How had Sereena turned against them? What could have driven her to such an act? His thoughts were interrupted as he rounded a corner and saw Catherine, crumpled on the ground, unconscious from the shock.

He fell to his knees beside her, his hands trembling as he checked for a pulse. Relief washed over him when he felt the steady beat beneath his fingers. "Catherine, wake up," he pleaded, his voice breaking. "I need you."

Tears streamed down his face as he cradled her in his arms, the weight of their situation pressing down on him. He couldn't do this alone. Their son needed them both, now more than ever. He took a deep breath, trying to steady his racing heart.

"Aurelius," came a voice from behind. He turned to see Xavier, his face pale with worry. "We need to get Catherine to safety. Then we'll find Caius."

Aurelius nodded, lifting Catherine into his arms. "Let's go," he said, his voice barely above a whisper.

They moved quickly, making their way to a safe house hidden in the heart of the city. As they entered, Martin/Aurelius laid Catherine gently on a couch, his eyes never leaving her face. "She'll be alright, "Xavier said softly. "She just needs time to recover."

Aurelius nodded, his thoughts already turning to their next move. "We need to find Sereena and Caius. There must be a reason for this. Something we're missing."

Xavier's eyes met his, filled with determination. "We'll find them, Aurelius. But we need to be smart about this. There's more at play here than we realize."

Chapter 7

As they strategist, the gravity of their situation became clear. Sereena's betrayal was part of a larger conspiracy, a web of deceit that threatened not just their family, but the entire planet. They had to uncover the truth and stop the malevolent force behind it.

Aurelius's thoughts were a whirlwind of fear and anger. How could Sereena, someone they trusted, do this? What was she after? He couldn't shake the feeling that they were missing a crucial piece of the puzzle.

Hours passed in a blur of planning and preparation. Catherine began to stir, her eyes fluttering open. "Martin?" she whispered; her voice weak.

"I'm here," he said, taking her hand in his. "We're going to find Caius, I promise."

Catherine's eyes filled with tears as she remembered the events that had unfolded. "Why would Sereena do this?" she asked, her voice trembling.

"I don't know," Martin/Aurelius replied, his voice filled with pain. "But we'll find out. And we'll bring our son home."

Xavier stood by the window, his eyes scanning the streets below. "We need to move quickly. If Sereena is part of a larger plan, we don't have much time."

Aurelius nodded, his mind racing with possibilities, Leo and Balendin arrived to assist they needed to uncover the truth behind Sereena's actions. Xander stayed with Catherine.

Deep down Balendin know this was not Sereena, she would never do something like this, there must be another reasonable answer.

As they prepared to leave, Martin/Aurelius felt a surge of determination. He wouldn't rest until his family was safe. They would face whatever came their way, together.

The journey to uncover the conspiracy took them deep into the heart of Xyphoria Prime. The city, usually vibrant and full of life, seemed overshadowed by an ominous presence.

Aurelus mind was a whirlwind of emotions. The betrayal, the fear for his son, the determination to protect his family—it all fueled his resolve. They had to succeed. Failure was not an option.

As they delved deeper into the conspiracy, they uncovered a sinister plot. A powerful force from Zamathia Vortex sought to destabilize Xyphoria Prime the timeline as well, using Sereena as a pawn in their game. The malevolent presence they had felt was just the beginning.

Aurelius heart ached with the weight of the truth. They were up against an enemy far more powerful and cunning than they had imagined. But they couldn't back down. Too much was at stake.

The final confrontation loomed on the horizon, each step bringing them closer to the heart of the darkness. Aurelius mind was filled with thoughts of Caius, his innocent face, his laughter. He couldn't let this happen. He had to save his son.

As they approached the outskirts of the city to a wilderness of forest and lushes' greenery, in the distance, they moved closer to see what was going on. Xavier saw a group in long flowing robes and some in cloaks adorned with intricate patterns and symbols that glow faintly.

Xavier insistently recognized them, they were Vortixians and here is their secret stronghold, the tension was palpable.

Aurelius turned to Xavier, "Who are these people?"

Xavier narrowed his eyes and remembered what they did to his people. They are vicious race that would stop at nothing to make them the powerful in the galaxy, like locusts, "Vortixians, they use dark magic, not very nice people."

Aurelius know bits about them from his father but still did not know enough, "They've been here before?"

Xavier bowed his head; he remembered the last conflict and that was when Aurelius went missing. Feeling the pain, he felt then, looked at Martin/Aurelius, "Yes, they blinded us so we would not see them and took you, right under our noses."

A fragment of memory came to Martin/Aurelius, he was in the playroom in the palace, there was a flash of light, and everything went dark. He was not going to let that happen to his son, history repeating itself.

Moving slowly forward Balendin caught a glimpse of Sereena she was in a same cloak as the others. He felt confused, why? Was she being blackmailed?

Leo gentle touched Balendin`s arm as tears started to well up in his eyes and spoke softly, "That's not her, Balendin, that's someone pretending to be her."

Balendin looked at Leo, "What do you mean?

Leo looked at the young woman, "She`s hollow, no soul."

Balendin was still confused but accepted what Leo was saying.

Aurelius and Balendin stood close together, their eyes fixed on Xavier as they entered the building undetected as he prepared for the final confrontation. Xavier's sword, a family heirloom passed down through generations, glowed with an ethereal light. Inscribed along its blade were ancient runes, their meanings known only to a select few.

As Xavier raised the sword, the runes began to shimmer, the words coming to life with a power that filled the room. He recited the incantation, his voice resonant with authority and ancient wisdom.

"Lux perpetua, tenebras disperge, custodi amorem et fortitudinem."

The words echoed in the chamber, their magic amplifying Xavier's strength and resolve. Translated, they meant, "Eternal light, disperse the darkness, guard love and strength." As the Vortixians detected them.

As the runes glowed brighter, a wave of light emanated from the sword, pushing back the encroaching shadows. The malevolent force from Zamathia Vortex recoiled, its dark tendrils retreating before the power of the incantation.

The light from Xavier's sword illuminated the room, revealing Sereena, true face was reviled, Leo was right it wasn't Sereena it was a Vortixian who disguised themselves to get close to Martin/Aurelius. Martin's heart ached for Balendin as the realization hit him, but his focus remained on the task at hand. They needed to neutralize the threat and save Caius.

Xavier, his face set with determination, stepped forward, the sword held high. "By the power of our ancestors, I command you to leave this place!" he shouted, his voice filled with unwavering resolve.

The dark force writhed, its presence a malevolent shadow against the brilliance of the sword's light. Martin/Aurelius could feel the tension in the air, the clash of light and darkness a battle for the very soul of Xyphoria Prime.

Leo, his eyes glowing with her own inner power, stepped forward to join Xavier. "We stand united against the darkness," she declared, her voice harmonizing with the magical energy in the room.

Aurelius found Caius and held him tight; he remembered the spell that Xaiver had told him prior to say. added their voices to the chorus. "Love and strength will prevail," he chanted, their words a testament to their unbreakable bond.

The combined power of their voices, the light of Xavier's sword, and the magic of Leo's abilities surged together, forming a barrier against the darkness. The malevolent force from Zamathia Vortex howled in defiance, but it could not withstand the united strength of their love and determination.

With a final, agonizing scream, the darkness dissipated, leaving the room bathed in the warm, comforting glow of the sword's light. The battle was over. They had triumphed.

Aurelius rushed to Balendin, his heart aching for him. "We will find Sereena, it's over for now."

Balendin looked at him, tears streaming down his face and trying to compose himself. "I'm so sorry, Aurelius."

He pulled him into a tight embrace. "We'll get through this together. We're family."

As they stood together, united in their victory, Martin/Aurelius felt a deep sense of peace as he held Caius. They had faced the darkness and emerged stronger for now, the final battle was yet to come, their bonds of love and strength unbreakable. Martin/Aurelius has also felt the family was everything and united as long as you have love and knew that no matter what challenges lay ahead.

Aurelius turned to Xavier to thank him, still leaning about his family asked, "What does your sword say?"

Xavier smiled as he flicked his sword up, "The magic words inscribed "Lux perpetua, tenebras disperge, custodi amorem et fortitudinem, meaning Eternal light, disperse the darkness, guard love and strength."

Aurelius reflected the battle, as they returned to the palace, the air filled with the clash of Xavier's weapon and the cries of the wounded and how he fought with everything he had; his mind focused on one goal: saving the timeline and Caius who was in a dark chamber, bound and terrified. Remembering how his heart broke at the sight of his son, but he pushed aside his pain. "Aeneas, it's going to be alright," he said, his voice filled with love and reassurance.

Aurelius, Balendin and Xavier know the danger was not over. The malevolent force from Zamathia Vortex still loomed, its presence a dark shadow, they still needed to rescue Sereena.

The enemy was defeated for now, and Xyphoria Prime was safe once more and timeline.

Aurelius placed Caius on the bed next Catherine, she woke her face full of joy as she wrapped her arms around Caius kissing him uncontrollable saying, "Am never going to let you out of my sight again."

Catherine held her arm out to Aurelius to beckon him closer, Aurelius knelt and wrapped his arms around both with tears streaming down his face as he cuddled his family.

Catherine's eyes filled with tears of joy. "We're a family," she said, her voice trembling. "And nothing will ever tear us apart."

Aurelius leaned in to kiss his wife and child feeling complete pride.

Chapter 8

As the two moons appeared stronger in the night skies, illuminating the planet with a cascade of shooting stars, Aurelius and Catherine cuddled on the balcony, looking up in awe. The night air was crisp and cool, a gentle breeze carrying the scents of the exotic flora that adorned Xyphoria Prime. It was a serene contrast to the chaos they had recently endured, a moment of peace that felt almost otherworldly.

Aurelius held Catherine close, feeling the steady rhythm of her heartbeat against his chest. The sight of the moons, their soft light casting a gentle glow over the landscape, filled him with a sense of calm. He could feel the weight of the past few weeks beginning to lift, replaced by a profound appreciation for this moment of tranquility.

"The sky is beautiful tonight," Catherine whispered, her voice soft and filled with wonder. She turned her gaze from the celestial display to Aurelius, her eyes reflecting the light of the moons. "It's like the universe is celebrating with us."

Aurelius smiled, brushing a strand of hair from her face. "It's magical," he agreed, his voice equally soft. "A reminder of all the beauty that's still out there, despite everything we've been through."

They sat in silence for a while, simply enjoying the beauty of the night. The stars seemed to dance across the sky, their movements graceful and mesmerizing. The moons, larger and more brilliant than ever, bathed the planet in their ethereal light. It was a sight that made the trials and tribulations they had faced feel like distant memories, if only for a moment.

As they watched, Aurelius's mind wandered back to the events that had brought them here. The fear, the danger, the uncertainty, it all seemed to fade in the light of the present. He thought of Caius, now safely asleep inside, and felt a surge of gratitude. They had faced the darkness and emerged stronger; their bonds unbroken.

Catherine's voice broke through his reverie. "What are you thinking about?" she asked, her tone gentle.

"Everything," he replied honestly. "How far we've come, how much we've faced. And how grateful I am to have you by my side."

She smiled, resting her head on his shoulder. "I feel the same way. It's been a long journey, but we're stronger for it."

Aurelius nodded, tightening his hold on her. "We are. And no matter what comes next, I know we can face it together."

The night continued to unfold, each moment bringing a new display of celestial beauty. They watched as the shooting stars streaked across the sky, their trails of light leaving a lasting impression on the darkness. The air was filled with the sounds of the night—distant calls of nocturnal creatures, the rustling of leaves, and the gentle hum of the planet's natural rhythms.

Catherine sighed contentedly; her eyes closed as she leaned into Martin's/Aurelius embrace. "This is perfect," she murmured. "Just us, the stars, and the promise of a new day."

Aurelius kissed the top of her head, his heart swelling with love. "It's more than I could have ever hoped for."

As the night wore on, they continued to talk, their conversation flowing effortlessly from one topic to the next. They spoke of their hopes and dreams, their fears and uncertainties. Each word was a thread, weaving them closer together, reinforcing the strength of their bond.

"I never imagined we'd end up here," Catherine said at one point, her voice tinged with wonder. "On a different planet, fighting against unimaginable forces."

Martin/Aurelius chuckled softly. "Life has a way of surprising us. But I wouldn't trade it for anything."

She looked up at him, her eyes filled with love. "Me neither. We've built something beautiful, despite everything."

He nodded; his heart full. "And we'll keep building. Together."

The hours passed, the moons continuing their journey across the sky. As dawn approached, the first hints of light began to touch the horizon, casting a soft glow over the landscape. The stars began to fade, their brilliance giving way to the new day.

Aurelius and Catherine stayed on the balcony, watching as the world around them came to life. The night air, once cool and crisp, began to warm, carrying the promise of a new beginning. It was a moment of renewal, a chance to start fresh, with the lessons of the past guiding them forward.

As the sun rose, its light mingling with the remnants of the moon's glow, Aurelius felt a sense of peace settle over him. The future was uncertain, but he was ready to face it, with Catherine and Caius by his side. They had overcome so much, and he knew they could handle whatever came next.

He turned to Catherine, his heart full of love and gratitude. "Let's go inside," he said softly. "A new day is starting, and we have a lot to look forward to."

She nodded, her eyes shining with hope. "Yes, we do."

Together, they rose and made their way inside, ready to embrace the new day and all the possibilities it held. The journey ahead was unknown, but they would face it together, their hearts intertwined, their love unbreakable.

As they stepped into the warmth of their home, Aurelius felt a sense of contentment wash over him. The challenges they had faced had brought them closer, forging a bond that was stronger than ever. And with that bond, they could face anything.

The days that followed were filled with a renewed sense of purpose. Aurelius and Catherine, along with their allies, continued to work towards rebuilding and strengthening their world. The lessons they had learned, the battles they had fought, all served to guide them as they moved forward.

There were moments of struggle, times when the weight of their responsibilities felt overwhelming. But through it all, they had each other, and that made all the difference.

As the evening draw in, they sat together watching the sunset, Catherine turned to Aurelius, her eyes filled with a quiet determination. "We've come so far," she said softly. "And we have so much more to do."

He nodded, his hand finding hers. "We do. But I have no doubt we can do it. Together."

She smiled, leaning into him. "Together," she echoed.

As the sun dipped below the horizon, casting the world in a warm, golden light, Aurelius felt a sense of peace. The future was theirs to shape, and with Catherine and Caius by his side, he knew they could create something beautiful.

The night air was filled with the promise of new beginnings, and as they sat there, basking in the warmth of their love, Aurelius knew that no matter what challenges lay ahead, they would face them together, their hearts forever bound by the strength of their bond.

And as the stars began to appear once more, twinkling in the night sky, he made a silent promise to himself: to cherish every moment, to love fiercely, and to never take for granted the incredible gift of his family.

The journey was far from over, but with Catherine and Caius by his side, Aurelius knew that anything was possible. Together, they would continue to build a future filled with hope, love, and endless possibilities.

As the two moons rose once more, casting their gentle light over the world, Aurelius held Catherine close, feeling the steady beat of her heart against his. The night air was cool and crisp, filled with the sounds of life and the promise of new beginnings.

And in that moment, he knew that they were exactly where they were meant to be together, on Xyphoria Prime and wondered if Catherine would be willing to give up life on Earth and live here.

For in the light of the moons, under the vast expanse of the star-filled sky, Aurelius realized that home was not a place, but a feeling, it's a feeling of love, of belonging, of being exactly where he was meant to be.

And if they had each other, they would always find their way home.

Chapter 9

The morning light filtered through the curtains as Aurelius slowly woke, the events of the past days weighing heavily on his mind. He turned to see Catherine still asleep beside him, her face peaceful despite the turmoil surrounding them. He knew they had to face another daunting challenge today.

A knock at the bedroom door pulled him from his thoughts. "Morning, Aurelius," came Balendin's voice, sounding both determined and anxious. "We are gathering in the throne room to discuss the plan to go to Zamathia Vortex to rescue Sereena."

Aurelius heart skipped a beat. The mission to rescue Sereena was fraught with danger, and the stakes were incredibly high. He carefully got out of bed, not wanting to disturb Catherine. "I'll be right there," he called out, trying to infuse his voice with confidence.

As he dressed, Aurelius couldn't help but feel a mix of emotions—fear, determination, and a deep sense of responsibility. Sereena's abduction had sent ripples through their lives, and now they were on the brink of a perilous mission to bring her back. He glanced at Catherine once more, drawing strength from her presence, before heading to the throne room.

Aurelius made his way through endless corridors and stairs and eventually arrived; the room was already bustling with activity. Balendin stood at the center, his face a mask of resolve but his eyes betraying the fear and anxiety he felt for Sereena. The weight of their mission was clearly pressing down on him, but his love for Sereena fueled his determination.

"Thank you all for coming," Balendin began, his voice steady despite the tension in the air. "We have a difficult journey ahead of us, but we cannot leave Sereena in the hands of those who seek to harm her. We must rescue her from Zamathia Vortex."

Aurelius stepped forward, placing a reassuring hand on Balendin's shoulder. "We will bring her back," he said firmly. "But we need a solid plan. How are we going to get there?"

Xavier, standing nearby, spoke up. "We have two options: we can travel by spaceship, which would be faster but risk detection, or we can use time travel, which would allow us to arrive undetected but is more complicated and riskier."

The room fell silent as they considered the options. Both methods had their merits and dangers, and the decision was crucial. Aurelius felt the weight of leadership pressing down on him, knowing that every choice carried significant consequences.

"We need to consider our allies," Leo said, his voice thoughtful. "We have support from other worlds, but we need to coordinate with them. We cannot face this threat alone."

As they discussed their strategy, the door to the throne room opened, and an imposing figure entered. It was King Orion, Sereena's father, ruler of Elysia. His presence commanded respect, and the room fell silent in acknowledgement of his power and authority.

"Thank you for coming, King Orion," Balendin said, bowing slightly. "Your support means everything to us."

King Orion nodded, his expression grave. "Sereena is my daughter, and her safety is paramount. Elysia stands with you in this mission.

We have powerful resources at our disposal, and we will use them to ensure her safe return."

Aurelius felt a surge of hope. With the support of King Orion and the might of Elysia, their chances of success were significantly higher. King Orion's realm was known for its advanced technology and powerful magic, making them formidable allies.

"We need to act quickly," Aurelius said, his voice resolute. "Time is of the essence. I suggest we use a combination of both methods, spaceships for speed and time travel for the final approach to avoid detection."

Xavier nodded in agreement. "I can handle the time travel aspect. It will be complex, but with the right preparations, we can make it work."

The plan began to take shape, each member of the team contributing their expertise. The room buzzed with a sense of urgency and determination. They mapped out their route, coordinated with their allies from other worlds, and prepared for the journey ahead.

As the preparations continued, Aurelius took a moment to speak with Balendin privately. "How are you holding up?" he asked, his voice filled with concern.

Balendin sighed, running a hand through his hair. "I'm scared, Aurelius. I can't lose her. But I know we must do this. For Sereena."

Aurelius placed a reassuring hand on Balendin's shoulder. "We'll get her back. I promise."

With the plan in place, they gathered their gear and prepared to depart and regroup in a couple of days, just to make it solid and let Vortixians believe they've given up. The sense of camaraderie and shared purpose was palpable, each person ready to do whatever it took to rescue Sereena. They boarded their ships, the engines humming with a sense of urgency.

Xavier explained the journey to Zamathia Vortex will be tense, each passing moment filled with anticipation and anxiety. Aurelius couldn't help but think of Catherine and Caius, hoping they would stay safe until he returned. He pushed those thoughts aside, focusing on the task at hand.

Chapter 10

Xavier stood on the balcony of the royal palace; his eyes fixed on the distant horizon. The events of the past days had taken a toll on him, and he found himself lost in memories of his home planet, Elaria. The beauty of Elaria was unparalleled, its skies a tapestry of colors, its landscapes lush and vibrant.

Elaria was home to the Guardians, a race of protectors trained to defend the realm from any threat. Xavier had been one of the most promising among them, his magic powerful and his resolve unwavering. The Guardians were revered for their abilities, their connection to the ancient magic that flowed through Elaria.

He remembered the day he had left Elaria, the sky filled with the light of a thousand stars. It had been a difficult decision, but necessary. The Vortixians had nearly destroyed his beautiful planet, their dark forces overwhelming the Guardians despite their best efforts. Xavier had been tasked with finding allies, a mission that had brought him to Xyphoria Prime.

The memories of Elaria were bittersweet. He missed the gentle hum of magic in the air, the sense of purpose that had guided him. But he knew that his journey had brought him to where he was needed most. The people of Xyphoria Prime had become his new family, and he was determined to protect them at all costs.

As he stood there, lost in thought, Martin/Aurelius joined him on the balcony. "Thinking about home?" Martin/Aurelius' asked, his voice gentle.

Xavier nodded, a wistful smile on his face. "Yes. Elaria was a place of great beauty and power. I miss it sometimes, but I know my place is here now."

Aurelius placed a hand on Xavier's shoulder, his eyes filled with understanding. "Your strength and magic have been invaluable to us. We couldn't have done this without you."

Xavier's smile grew, his heart warmed by Aurelius's words. "Thank you, Aurelius. That means a lot."

The two men stood in companionable silence, the bond between them strengthened by their shared experiences. The night air was cool and refreshing, a gentle breeze carrying the scent of the ocean.

As the dawn began to break, casting a golden light over the horizon, Xavier felt a renewed sense of purpose. They had faced incredible challenges and emerged victorious, their unity and determination carrying them through. And with the support of his new family, he knew they could face anything.

The memories of Elaria would always be with him, a reminder of where he had come from and the strength that lay within him. But his heart now belonged to Xyphoria Prime, and he would do whatever it took to protect it.

With a final glance at the horizon, Xavier turned to Aurelius, his eyes filled with determination. "We have a lot of work ahead of us. But I know we can do it. Together."

Aurelius nodded, his heart swelling with pride and gratitude. "Together," he echoed, knowing that their bond would guide them through whatever challenges lay ahead.

As they walked back inside, ready to face the new day, Xavier felt a deep sense of peace. He was a Guardian, a protector of the realm, and with his new family by his side, he knew that anything was possible.

The future was filled with uncertainty, but it was also filled with hope. And as they looked to the horizon, they knew that they would face it together, their hearts united by a shared purpose and an unbreakable bond.

The days that followed were filled with preparation and planning. They knew that the Vortixians were still a threat, and they could not afford to let their guard down. Xavier's knowledge of Elarian magic proved invaluable, his training as a Guardian guiding their efforts to strengthen their defenses and prepare for any future attacks.

The people of Xyphoria Prime rallied together, their spirits bolstered by the recent victory and the promise of a brighter future. The sense of unity and determination was palpable, each person playing their part in the collective effort to protect their home.

Xavier found himself reflecting on his journey, the challenges he had faced, and the people who had become his family. He felt a deep sense of gratitude for the bonds they had forged and the strength they had found in each other.

One evening, as the sun set over the horizon, casting a warm golden light over the city, Xavier stood with Aurelius, Catherine, and the rest of their allies. They watched as the stars began to appear, twinkling in the night sky like beacons of hope.

"We've come a long way," Aurelius said softly, his eyes fixed on the stars.

Catherine nodded, her eyes filled with love and determination. "And we have so much more to do. But I know we can face anything together."

Xavier felt a surge of pride and gratitude. "We are stronger together," he said, his voice filled with conviction. "And we will protect our home, no matter what."

As they stood together, united by a shared purpose and an unbreakable bond, the night air was filled with the promise of new beginnings and endless possibilities. They had faced incredible challenges and emerged victorious, their love and determination guiding them through the darkest of times.

And as they looked to the future, they knew that they could face anything together, their hearts united by a shared purpose and an unbreakable bond.

Balendin stood in silence listening to the chatter when his mind cast back how he met Sereena and her family.

Chapter 11

Balendin remembered standing on the balcony of royal palace on Elysia, gazing out over the lush landscapes of Elysia. As he's mind drifted back to the first time he had met Sereena. It had been a day that changed his life forever, a moment etched in his memory with the vividness of a dream.

He had been invited to a grand ball at the palace, a celebration of Elysia's annual festival of lights. The evening was magical, the palace adorned with thousands of glowing lanterns that illuminated the night sky. Balendin had felt a mix of excitement and nervousness as he entered the grand hall, the air filled with laughter and music.

And then he saw her. Sereena stood at the center of the room, her presence radiant. She was talking with a group of dignitaries, her smile lighting up the room. Balendin's heart skipped a beat. It was love at first sight. He couldn't take his eyes off her, captivated by her grace and beauty.

Gathering his courage, he approached her. "Excuse me, Princess Sereena," he said, his voice steady despite his racing heart. "May I have this dance?"

Sereena turned to him, her eyes sparkling with curiosity. "Of course," she replied, her smile warm and inviting.

As they danced, Balendin felt an undeniable connection between them. They moved effortlessly together, their bodies in perfect harmony with the music. He found himself lost in her eyes, the world around them fading into the background.

After the dance, they talked for hours, sharing stories and laughter. Balendin discovered that Sereena was not only beautiful but also kind and intelligent. Her passion for her people and her dedication to her duties as a princess left him in awe.

Their conversation was interrupted by the arrival of Sereena's adopted brother, Liber. Balendin found him odd, his demeanour distant and aloof. There was something unsettling about him, a darkness that lingered just beneath the surface. Despite this, Sereena spoke of him with affection, and Balendin knew better than to voice his concerns.

Over the following weeks, Balendin and Sereena grew closer. They spent every moment they could together, exploring the beautiful landscapes of Elysia, sharing dreams and aspirations. Each day brought new adventures and unforgettable moments.

There was one day that stood out in Balendin's memory. They had decided to visit a secluded waterfall deep within the forest. The journey was challenging, but Sereena's spirit and enthusiasm made it a joy. When they finally arrived, the sight took Balendin's breath away. The waterfall cascaded down into a crystal-clear pool, the sound of the rushing water soothing and invigorating.

They swam in the pool, laughing and splashing each other like children. As they sat on the rocks, drying off in their two Suns, Sereena leaned close to Balendin and whispered, "This is perfect. I wish we could stay here forever."

Balendin looked into her eyes, his heart swelling with love. "Me too," he replied, pulling her into a tender kiss. It was a moment of pure bliss, a memory he would cherish forever.

Their love blossomed, each day deepening their bond. Balendin knew he wanted to spend the rest of his life with Sereena. His passion for her was overwhelming, a fire that burned brightly in his heart.

But there were challenges ahead. Liber's odd behaviour continued to trouble Balendin, and he couldn't shake the feeling that something was amiss. Sereena's father, King Orion, was a powerful ruler, respected and feared throughout the realm. Balendin knew he had to prove himself worthy of Sereena's love and trust.

The day Balendin decided to ask for King Orion's blessing was one of the most nerve-wracking of his life. He stood before the king, his heart pounding. "Your Majesty," he began, his voice steady despite his nerves. "I love your daughter, Sereena, with all my heart. I wish to spend my life with her, to protect and cherish her. I humbly ask for your blessing."

King Orion regarded Balendin with a stern expression, his eyes penetrating. After what felt like an eternity, the king's face softened, and he nodded. "You have my blessing, Balendin. Treat her well, and you will always have my support."

Relief and joy washed over Balendin. He thanked the king profusely, his heart soaring. With King Orion's blessing, he felt invincible, ready to face any challenge that came their way.

Their love story was filled with breathtaking moments and passionate declarations. Balendin and Sereena were inseparable, their bond unbreakable. But beneath the surface, a darker story was unfolding, one that would soon come to light back on Xyphria Prime.

Chapter 12

Liber had always been an enigma, a puzzle that no one could quite solve. Adopted by King Orion as a baby, he had grown up alongside Sereena, his presence a constant in her life. But there was a darkness in Liber, a sinister edge that set him apart. The truth about Liber's origins was a closely guarded secret. His real father was Icarus, a powerful and malevolent Vortixian. Icarus had left Liber on Elysia as a baby, knowing that King Orion, a man of great honour and compassion, would raise him as his own. It was a calculated move, part of a larger plan that had been years in the making.

Liber had been a spy for his father, gathering information and subtly influencing events to further Icarus's goals. He had always felt a deep, conflicted loyalty—towards King Orion and Sereena, who had both shown him kindness and love, and towards his real father, whose shadow loomed large over his life.

It was during his time as a spy that Liber met Aurora. She was tall and slim, with flowing blonde hair and piercing blue eyes. Her beauty was almost otherworldly, her presence commanding attention wherever she went. Aurora was an operative for the Keepers of Time, a secretive organization dedicated to maintaining the integrity of the timeline.

Liber was instantly captivated by her, drawn to her strength and intelligence. They began a passionate affair, their love burning bright and intense. But Aurora was not easily deceived. She sensed that Liber was hiding something, and her instincts told her to be cautious.

As their relationship deepened, Aurora began to uncover the truth about Liber. She discovered his connection to Icarus and his role as a spy. The revelation was devastating, shattering her trust and breaking her heart.

Confronting Liber, Aurora's voice trembled with emotion. "How could you do this? Everything we've built, everything we shared—was it all a lie?"

Liber's face was a mask of anguish. "Aurora, I love you. But my loyalty to my father is something I cannot deny."

Aurora's eyes filled with tears. "You have to choose Liber. Me or him. You can't have both."

The conflict tore Liber apart. He couldn't bear the thought of losing Aurora, but he also couldn't betray his father. The tension between them grew, their once passionate love now fraught with distrust and pain.

In the end, Aurora made the choice for him. She left, her heart heavy with sorrow. "I can't be with someone I can't trust," she said, her voice breaking. "Goodbye, Liber."

The breakup left Liber devastated, his heart shattered. He threw himself into his work, his actions becoming more ruthless and driven by his father's ambitions. The darkness within him grew, his sinister side coming to the forefront.

But fate had other plans. Balendin and the others managed to uncover Liber's identity and his connection to Icarus. They captured him in 1983, just before he could carry out a series of murders of innocent young women. The relief and satisfaction Balendin felt were immense. They had stopped a great evil, preventing unimaginable suffering.

As Liber was taken away, Balendin couldn't help but feel a sense of pity for him. Despite everything, Liber was a product of his circumstances, a pawn in his father's cruel game. But justice had been served, and the future was a little brighter for it.

With Liber's capture, the threat of Icarus and his malevolent plans remained. But Balendin, Sereena, and their allies were stronger than ever, united by their love and determination. They knew there would be more challenges ahead, but they were ready to face them together.

The past had shaped them, but the future was theirs to build. And as they moved forward, they did so with the knowledge that their love was the greatest power of all, a beacon of light in even the darkest times. In the early days of their relationship, Liber and Aurora shared moments of vulnerability that neither had experienced before. Liber, often closed off and guarded, found solace in Aurora's presence. She had a way of making him feel seen and understood in ways that no one else ever had.

One evening, under the starlit sky, Liber opened to Aurora about his fears and insecurities. "I sometimes feel like I'm living someone else's life," he admitted, his voice barely above a whisper. "The weight of my father's expectations, the secrets I keep... it's like I'm drowning."

Aurora reached out, her fingers gently intertwining with his. "You don't have to carry this burden alone, Liber. I'm here for you. Always."

In those moments, Liber felt a warmth and safety he had never known. He began to share more with Aurora, revealing the softer sides of himself that he had long kept hidden. They would spend hours talking, laughing, and sometimes just sitting in comfortable silence, their connection deepening with each passing day.

Aurora, too, found herself opening to Liber. She shared stories of her childhood, her dreams, and her fears. Together, they created a world where they could be their true selves, free from the shadows of their pasts. Their love was a sanctuary, a place where they could heal and grow.

However, the shadow of Icarus always loomed over Liber, creating a tension that neither could fully escape. Despite their love, the secrets and lies began to weigh heavily on Aurora. She started noticing the cracks in Liber's facade, the moments of hesitation and guilt that hinted at the truth.

One night, after a particularly heated argument, Aurora couldn't hold back any longer. "Why won't you let me in, Liber? What are you so afraid of?"

Liber's eyes were filled with pain. "I'm afraid of losing you, Aurora. Afraid that if you knew the truth, you'd hate me."

Tears streamed down Aurora's face. "I don't want lies, Liber. I want you—all of you. The good, the bad, the ugly. We can't build a life together on half-truths and secrets."

Despite his fear, Liber took a deep breath and began to share the truth about his past, his father, and his role as a spy. With each revelation, Aurora's heart broke a little more, but she listened, her love for him battling with her sense of betrayal.

When he finished, Aurora's voice was a mixture of sorrow and resolve. "I love you, Liber. But I can't be with someone I can't trust. You have to decide what kind of man you want to be."

The choice tore Liber apart. He knew he couldn't continue living a double life but breaking free from his father's grip seemed impossible. In the end, Aurora made the decision for him, walking away with a heavy heart, leaving Liber to grapple with his choices and the path he would take.

Liber's love for Aurora had awakened something in him a desire to be better, to break free from the darkness that had consumed him. Her departure left a void that nothing could fill, but it also ignited a spark of hope. For the first time, Liber began to question his loyalty to his father and consider the possibility of a different future.

As he navigated the complex web of his emotions, Liber found himself reflecting on the moments he had shared with Aurora. The way her laughter could light up a room, the gentleness of her touch, the way she believed in him even when he couldn't believe in himself. These memories became his guiding light, pushing him to seek redemption and a chance to rewrite his story.

In the end, it was Aurora's love and the hope it inspired that led Liber to make the hardest decision of his life. He chose to turn to his father, to fight for a future where he could be seen and heard, headed to the shadows of his past. It was a long and difficult journey.

Chapter 13

Balendin reached the balcony other side of the royal palace to be alone, stared out into the vast expanse of Xyphoria Prime. The moons hung low in the sky, casting a silvery glow over the landscape dawn was nearly up in a few hours. The sight was beautiful, but it did little to soothe the ache in his heart. He missed Sereena more than words could express, his longing for her presence consuming his thoughts.

He closed his eyes, imagining the feel of her soft skin against his, the warmth of her embrace, and the sweetness of her lips. The memories of their time together played like a bittersweet symphony in his mind, each note a reminder of what he was fighting for.

The royal bodysuit he wore was a testament to his status and heritage. The fabric clung to his form, a perfect blend of comfort and reality. The flowing cape that adorned his shoulders was a marvel of technology, holographic patterns shifting and changing with every movement. Sometimes it displayed scenes from Xyphoria Prime's rich history battles fought and won, moments of peace and prosperity. Other times, it showcased abstract, futuristic designs that were a nod to the innovation and creativity of his people. A small crown rested on his head, a symbol of his lineage and his responsibilities.

But today, even the grandeur of his attire couldn't lift his spirits. He missed Sereena with an intensity that bordered on physical pain. Her absence was a void that nothing could fill. He longed to feel her touch, to hear her voice, to hold her close and never let go.

As he stood lost in thought, he heard footsteps approaching. He turned to see Aurelius entering the balcony. Aurelius presence was a welcome distraction, and Balendin managed a small smile.

"Morning, Balendin," Aurelius greeted, his tone light.

"Good morning, Aurelius," Balendin replied, trying to mask the heaviness in his heart.

Aurelius wore his usual Earth attire, a stark contrast to the elaborate clothing of Xyphoria Prime. Balendin chuckled, remembering the incident earlier that day when Martin had outright refused to wear the royal bodysuit.

"Come on, Aurelius," Balendin had urged, holding up the intricate garment. "It's tradition."

Aurelius had eyed the suit with a mix of horror and amusement. "There is no way I'm wearing that. I can barely move in my own clothes, let alone something that looks like it belongs in a sci-fi movie."

Catherine had laughed, stepping forward in her own Xyphorian attire. She embraced the style with grace and elegance, the holographic patterns on her cape adding an ethereal quality to her appearance. "I think it's beautiful," she had said, twirling to show off the shifting designs. "You should give it a try, Aurelius."

But Aurelius had shaken his head, his expression resolute. "Nope. Not happening."

The memory brought a genuine smile to Balendin's face, a brief respite from his sorrow. Aurelius refusal to conform to Xyphorian fashion had provided a moment of levity, a reminder that even in the darkest times, there was still room for laughter.

"You're thinking about her, aren't you?" Aurelius voice brought Balendin back to the present.

Balendin sighed, nodding. "Every moment. I can't help it. The thought of her out there, alone and in danger... it's unbearable."

Aurelius placed a reassuring hand on Balendin's shoulder. "We'll find her. I promise you; we'll bring her back."

Balendin appreciated the sentiment, but the weight of uncertainty still pressed heavily on his heart. "I know we will," he said, his voice tinged with a mixture of hope and despair. "I just wish it could be sooner."

They stood in silence for a moment, the night/dawn air cool against their skin. Balendin's thoughts drifted back to the early days of his relationship with Sereena, the joy and excitement of their blossoming love.

He remembered the day they had met, the instant connection he had felt. It was as if the universe had aligned to bring them together. Every moment with her had been magical, from the grandest adventures to the simplest conversations.

One memory stood out, a day they had spent exploring an ancient forest on the outskirts of Xyphoria Prime. They had wandered through the towering trees, their laughter echoing through the quiet woods. At one point, Sereena had stumbled upon a hidden grove filled with flowers of every color imaginable. She had turned to Balendin, her eyes sparkling with delight.

"Isn't it beautiful?" she had whispered, her voice filled with wonder.

Balendin had been mesmerized, not by the flowers, but by her. "Yes," he had replied, his gaze locked on her. "Absolutely breathtaking."

They had spent hours in that grove, talking, laughing, and simply enjoying each other's company. It was one of those perfect days that stayed with you forever, a moment of pure happiness that nothing could tarnish.

Balendin longed to create more memories like that with Sereena. He wanted to spend the rest of his life making her smile, sharing in her joys and supporting her through her sorrows. The thought of losing her was more than he could bear.

"We'll get her back," Aurelius repeated, his voice firm. "We'll face whatever comes, and we'll do it together."

Balendin nodded, drawing strength from Aurelius resolve. They had faced countless challenges already, and they would face many more. But with friends like Aurelius his brother and the love he felt for Sereena, he knew they could overcome anything.

As the night wore on, the two men continued to talk, their conversation a mix of strategy and reminiscence. Balendin found solace in the company of his friend, brother, a reminder that he was not alone in this struggle.

When they finally parted ways, Balendin felt a renewed sense of determination. He would not rest until Sereena was safe. His love for her was a beacon, guiding him through the darkness. And with the support of his family, friends and allies, he knew they would succeed.

Balendin returned to his quarters, the weight of his royal responsibilities pressing heavily on his shoulders. As he prepared for bed, he took a moment to look at a picture of Sereena, a small smile playing on his lips. "We'll be together again," he whispered, his voice filled with conviction. "I promise."

The next morning, the palace was a flurry of activity as preparations for their mission continued. Balendin donned his royal bodysuit, the holographic patterns shifting to display scenes from Xyphoria Prime's storied past. He stood tall, the small crown on his head a symbol of his duty and determination.

As he joined the others, he couldn't help but feel a sense of anticipation. The road ahead was fraught with danger, but he was ready. With

Sereena's love as his guiding light, he would face whatever challenges came their way.

The journey to rescue Sereena was about to begin, and Balendin was prepared to give everything he had. He would fight for her, for their future, and for the love that bound them together. And with the support of his friends and allies, he knew they would succeed.

As they set out on their mission, Balendin felt a surge of hope. The path was uncertain, but his love for Sereena was unwavering. They would find her, they would bring her back, and they would face the future together, stronger than ever before.

With each step he took, Balendin's resolve grew stronger. He was ready to face whatever challenges lay ahead, fueled by the love he felt for Sereena and the determination to protect her at all costs. The future was uncertain, but he knew that with the support of his friends, family and the strength of his love, they could overcome anything.

And as they embarked on their journey, Balendin felt a deep sense of purpose. They were fighting for more than just their lives, they were fighting for their love, their future, and the hope that one day, they would be reunited with the ones they cherished most.

Chapter 14

T he air in Xyphoria Prime was thick with tension as the looming battle with Zamathia Vortex drew closer. The citizens, usually vibrant and bustling with energy, moved with a palpable sense of apprehension. The impending conflict weighed heavily on their hearts and minds, casting a shadow over their once peaceful world.

Balendin stood at the center of the palace courtyard, his gaze fixed on the horizon. The weight of the upcoming battle pressed heavily on his shoulders. He felt a mix of fear and determination, his thoughts consumed by the need to rescue Sereena. Every moment without her was agony, and the thought of what she might be enduring drove him to the brink of despair.

Beside him, Xander's expression was grim. The seasoned warrior had seen countless battles, but the stakes had never been this high. His thoughts were a whirlwind of strategy and concern for his family. He glanced at Balendin, his heart aching for his son. The bond between them was unbreakable, and Xander vowed to do everything in his power to bring Sereena back safely.

Xavier stood nearby; his face etched with worry. The Guardian's connection to Elarian magic made him a vital asset, but even he could feel the oppressive weight of the situation. His mind raced with thoughts of the upcoming battle, the strategies they needed to employ, and the magic he would need to wield to protect those he cared about.

The memories of his home planet, nearly destroyed by the Vortixians, fuelled his determination to prevent such devastation from occurring again.

Aurelius paced back and forth, his thoughts a jumble of fear and resolve. The responsibility of leadership weighed heavily on him, and the safety of his family was paramount. He couldn't shake the image of Sereena, alone and in danger. The love he felt for Catherine and Aeneas drove him forward, pushing him to face his fears and fight for their future.

Isabella stood in quiet contemplation, her abilities as a medium providing glimpses of the possible futures that lay ahead. She felt the anxiety of the citizens and the fear of her friends, and it only strengthened her resolve. She had seen darkness and light, and she knew that their unity would be their greatest strength in the battle to come.

King Orion's presence commanded respect and reverence. The usually composed ruler was visibly shaken, the pain of his missing daughter etched into every line of his face. His heart ached for Sereena, his thoughts consumed by worry and fear. As the leader of Elysia, he had faced many challenges, but nothing compared to the anguish of not knowing his daughter's fate. He drew strength from his people and his allies, vowing to do whatever it took to bring Sereena home.

The courtyard was filled with representatives from other worlds who had joined the rescue mission. Their diverse appearances and attire were a testament to the unity and cooperation that had been forged in the face of a common enemy. Everyone carried their own fears and hopes, their resolve steeled by the knowledge that they were fighting for more than just themselves.

As the days passed, the tension only grew. The palace was a hive of activity, preparations for the battle consuming every moment. The citizens of Xyphoria Prime watched anxiously; their hearts heavy with the weight of the impending conflict. The usually serene streets were filled with whispers of fear and hope, each person clinging to the belief that their heroes would succeed.

Balendin spent long hours training and strategist, his thoughts never far from Sereena. He could almost feel her presence, a constant reminder of what they were fighting for. The nights were the hardest, the silence amplifying his fears. But he held onto the hope that they would be reunited, that their love would prevail against the darkness.

Xander and Xavier worked tirelessly, their combined experience and magic a crucial part of their preparations. They shared stories of past battles, drawing strength from each other's presence. The bond between them was a source of comfort and inspiration, a reminder that they were not alone in this fight.

Aurelius found solace in his family, their love a beacon of hope in the midst of the storm. He spent as much time as he could with Catherine and Caius, drawing strength from their presence. The thought of losing them was unbearable, and it fueled his determination to succeed.

Leo continued to provide guidance, his visions offering glimpses of the paths they could take. He felt the weight of responsibility, knowing that her insights could make the difference between victory and defeat. His calm presence was a source of comfort for those around him, a reminder that they were not facing this challenge alone.

King Orion's presence was a constant reminder of the stakes. His pain and determination were palpable, his love for Sereena driving him forward. He spent hours in the war room, strategist with his advisors and allies. The thought of rescuing his daughter was the only thing that kept him going, a glimmer of hope in the darkness.

As the day of the battle drew nearer, the tension reached its peak. The palace was filled with a sense of urgency, every moment precious.

The citizens of Xyphoria Prime watched with bated breath, their hopes and prayers with their heroes.

The night before the battle, the allies gathered for a final meeting. The room was filled with a sense of resolve and determination, each person ready to face the challenges ahead. They went over their plans one last time, ensuring that every detail was accounted for.

Balendin stood at the center of the room, his heart heavy with emotion. He looked around at the faces of his friends and allies, drawing strength from their presence. "Tomorrow, we face our greatest challenge," he began, his voice steady despite the fear that gnawed at his heart. "But we are not alone. We have each other, and we have the strength of our love and determination. We will rescue Sereena, and we will prevail."

The room erupted in a chorus of agreement; the resolve of each person unwavering. They knew that the battle ahead would be difficult, but they were ready. They had faced darkness before, and they would face it again.

As they dispersed, Balendin felt a sense of calm settle over him. The path ahead was uncertain, but he knew that they would face it together. The love he felt for Sereena was a beacon of hope, guiding him through the darkness. And with the support of his friends and allies, he knew that they would succeed.

Chapter 15

Balendin, Aurelius, and Leo gathered in the palace throne room, their expressions a mix of determination and apprehension. They had decided that it was time to pay Liber a visit in his dimensional prison. The hope was that he might have answers about why Icarus wanted Sereena and what his ultimate plans were.

The prison existed in a dimension far removed from their own, a place designed to contain the most dangerous of beings. The journey there required the use of a portal, an ancient and intricate device that would transport them across the boundaries of space and time.

"Are we ready?" Aurelius asked, his voice steady but his eyes betraying his concern.

Balendin nodded. "We need to understand what we're up against. Liber might be our only chance to get the information we need."

Xaviar, his eyes glowing with the faint light of his abilities, added, "I've prepared the portal. It should be stable, but we need to be cautious. Dimensional travel is unpredictable but remember he still could be a threat."

They moved to the center of the room where the portal stood, a shimmering vortex of light and energy. Taking a deep breath, they stepped through together.

The transition was disorienting, a whirlwind of colors and sounds that left them momentarily breathless. When they emerged, they found themselves in a desolate landscape, the sky a dark, swirling mass of clouds. The ground beneath them was barren and cracked, the air heavy with an oppressive energy.

The prison itself was a towering fortress of dark stone, its walls etched with runes of containment. Guards patrolled the perimeter, their expressions hard and unyielding. As Balendin, Aurelius, and Leo approached, the guards stepped aside, recognizing the significance of their visit.

Inside, the prison was a labyrinth of corridors and cells, each designed to suppress the powers of its inmates. They were led to a large chamber where Liber was being held. The room was stark, the only light coming from a small, barred window high above.

Liber looked up as they entered, his expression a mix of surprise and wariness. He was seated on a simple cot, his once imposing figure now seeming diminished and worn.

"The great Balendin, how's your nose? Martin, oops sorry Aurelius, the long-lost son and brother, oh the talented Leo," he greeted them, his voice lacking its usual arrogance. "To what do I owe this unexpected pleasure?"

Aurelius retooled back, "How's the shoulder, Liber?"

Liber narrowed his eyes as he remembered Aurelius shoot him, touching his shoulder, "It's fine."

Balendin stepped forward into the light in the center of the room, his eyes hard. "We need answers, Liber. Why does Icarus want Sereena? What are his plans?"

Liber sighed, running a hand through his hair. "Icarus... always playing his games," he muttered as he put one foot on the bed leaning on it. "He wants to disrupt the balance, to destroy The Keepers of Time and seize control of Xyphoria Prime and the surrounding planets. Sereena is a key part of his plan."

Aurelius crossed his arms, his expression skeptical. "Why should we believe you? How do we know you're not just playing us?"

A wry smile crossed Liber's face. "Look, I can't blame you for doubting me. I haven't exactly been trustworthy, have I?"

Leo's eyes narrowed as he focused on Liber, he could sense apart of him being sincere. "What do you gain from helping us?"

Liber's smile faded, replaced by a look of genuine remorse. "I've had a lot of time to think, here in this place. Time to realize the mistakes I've made. Icarus never loved me. He used me, manipulated me for his own ends. I see that now."

Balendin's anger softened slightly as he saw the pain in Liber's eyes. "And what about Sereena? Do you care about her at all?"

Liber's expression became distant, a hint of sadness in his eyes. "Sereena is my sister, even if not by blood. Of course I care about her. I never wanted her to be hurt."

Aurelius tone was more measured as he asked, "What about Aurora? Do you still want to see her?"

A flicker of longing passed over Liber's face. "Aurora... I never stopped loving her. Losing her was the hardest thing I've ever endured. She was the one good thing in my life, and I ruined it."

There was a moment of silence as they absorbed Liber's words. Despite their history, it was clear that he was struggling with genuine remorse.

"We need your help," Balendin said finally. "If you truly regret your actions, if you truly care about Sereena, then help us stop Icarus."

Liber looked up, his eyes filled with a mix of hope and fear. "I will help you. I don't want to be a pawn in Icarus's game any longer. I want to make things right."

The sincerity in Liber's voice was unmistakable, and for the first time, Balendin felt a flicker of hope. Maybe, just maybe, they could trust him.

"Thank you," Leo said softly. "We need to know everything you can tell us about Icarus's plans. How can we stop him?"

Liber nodded, his expression resolute. "I'll tell you everything I know. But we need to act quickly. Icarus's plans are already in motion."

As they listened to Liber's account, they began to piece together the full extent of Icarus's schemes. It was a plan of terrifying scope, aimed at unraveling the very fabric of their reality.

Despite the gravity of the situation, there were moments of unexpected levity. Liber's dry, sarcastic humor surfaced occasionally, a defense mechanism against the darkness he had endured.

"So, let me get this straight," Aurelius said with a raised eyebrow. "Your father's grand plan involves destabilizing multiple dimensions, enslaving entire worlds, and... what? Becoming the ultimate ruler of chaos?"

Liber snorted. "Pretty much. He always did have a flair for the dramatic."

Balendin couldn't help but chuckle. Despite everything, there was something almost absurd about Icarus's over-the-top villainy. It was a brief, much-needed moment of humour in an otherwise dire situation.

As they prepared to leave, Liber's expression became serious once more. "One more thing," he said, his voice soft. "When this is all over... if it's possible, I'd like to see Aurora again. I

need to apologize. To try to make things right. Before I forget you also will need my device that you took of me to entre Zamathia , we don't want you entering the Vortex of Shadows detected, do we now."

Balendin nodded, a sense of understanding passing between them. "We'll do everything we can. For now, let's focus on stopping Icarus."

They left the prison, their minds filled with the information Liber had provided. The path ahead was clearer now, but no less daunting. They had a plan, and they had an ally in Liber, but the stakes were higher than ever.

As they stepped through the portal and returned to Xyphoria Prime, Balendin felt a renewed sense of purpose. They would face the coming battle with everything they had. For Sereena, for their future, and for the chance to right the wrongs of the past.

The tension among the citizens and the allies from other worlds was palpable as the day of the battle approached. But there was also a sense of unity and determination. They were ready to face the darkness and fight for the light.

In the days leading up to the battle, Balendin, Martin, Xavier and Leo worked tirelessly, coordinating their efforts and refining their strategies. The support of their friends and allies bolstered their spirits, giving them the strength to keep pushing forward.

And through it all, Balendin held onto the hope that they would succeed. That they would rescue Sereena and bring her home. The journey ahead was fraught with danger, but they were ready to face it together, united by love and determination.

As the final preparations were made, Balendin took a moment to reflect on the path that had brought them here. It had been a journey of struggle and sacrifice, but also one of growth and resilience. They had faced their fears and come out stronger for it.

With the battle looming, they knew that the future was uncertain. But one thing was clear: they would fight with everything they had, for the people they loved and the world they wanted to protect. As they stood on the brink of the final confrontation, they felt a sense of calm amidst the storm. They were ready to face whatever came their way, their hearts united by a shared purpose and an unbreakable bond.

Chapter 16

The atmosphere in the throne room was tense as Balendin, Aurelius, and Leo returned from their visit to Liber. The weight of the information they had gathered hung heavily in the air, each of them processing the implications of what they had learned. King Orion, Xavier, and Xander awaited their report, their expressions a mix of anticipation and concern.

Balendin took a deep breath, steeling himself for the conversation ahead. "We've just returned from visiting Liber in his dimensional prison," he began, his voice steady but filled with urgency. "He's given us critical information about Icarus's plans and his interest in Sereena."

King Orion's eyes narrowed, his concern for his daughter evident. "What did he say?"

Aurelius stood next to Balendin, his tone serious. "Icarus wants to disrupt the balance, to destroy The Keepers of Time and seize control of Xyphoria Prime and the surrounding planets. Sereena is a key part of his plan."

Xavier leaned back in his chair, a sardonic smile playing on his lips. "Of course, the classic 'take over the universe' plan. Icarus must have missed the memo on originality."

Balendin couldn't help but chuckle at Xavier's remark, appreciating the moment of levity in the otherwise grim discussion. "Liber also mentioned that Icarus's ultimate goal is to control multiple dimensions, using the vortexes to his advantage."

Xander's face grew stern. "If that's true, we're dealing with a threat far greater than we anticipated. We need to act quickly and decisively."

Leo nodded, his expression thoughtful. "Liber seemed genuinely remorseful. He regrets his past actions and wants to make amends. He's willing to help us stop Icarus."

King Orion's expression softened slightly. "Did he say why he's had this change of heart?"

Balendin sighed. "He realized that Icarus never loved him, that he was just a pawn in his father's game. Liber wants to protect Sereena and make things right."

Xavier's sarcastic edge softened as he considered this. "Well, it's about time he had an epiphany. Better late than never, I suppose."

The room fell silent as they absorbed the gravity of the situation. The weight of their responsibility pressed down on them, each person processing the information in their own way.

King Orion broke the silence, his voice filled with determination. "We will rescue Sereena and stop Icarus or destroy him, one of the two. We have the information we need, and now we must act on it."

They spent the next hours meticulously going over their plans, ensuring that every detail was accounted for. The atmosphere in the room was charged with a mix of tension and resolve, each person focused on the task at hand.

Xavier, despite his earlier sarcasm, was a pillar of strength and strategy. His insights into Elarian magic and dimensional travel were invaluable, guiding their plans and providing a clear path forward.

As they finalized their preparations, Balendin felt a renewed sense of hope. They had a plan, and they had the support of their friends and allies. Together, they would face the coming battle and rescue Sereena.

Chapter 17

The journey to Zamathia Vortex was fraught with uncertainty and danger. The planet was a nightmarish landscape, dotted with vortexes that led to various dimensions. Dark clouds roiled across the sky, casting an eerie glow over the unstable terrain. The very ground seemed to shift and tremble, as if the planet itself was alive and struggling against the chaos.

Balendin, Martin/Aurelius, Isabella, Xander, Xavier, and King Orion gathered their forces and prepared to depart. They would use a vortex device provided by Liber, a complex piece of technology that allowed them to travel to Zamathia Vortex undetected.

The device was a small, intricately designed orb, pulsating with a soft, blue light. Liber had explained its function, detailing how it could create a temporary rift in space-time, allowing them to slip through the dimensional boundaries without alerting Icarus's forces.

As they activated the device, a portal shimmered into existence before them. The air crackled with energy, the edges of the portal flickering with an ethereal light. Taking a deep breath, they stepped through, the sensation akin to being pulled through a tunnel of swirling colors and sounds.

The journey through the vortex was disorienting, the fabric of reality bending and twisting around them. It felt like an eternity and an instant all at once. When they finally emerged on the other side, they found themselves on the surface of Zamathia Vortex.

The landscape was even more foreboding up close. The vortexes dotted the terrain like dark, swirling maws, each one a gateway to a different dimension. The sky above was a turbulent sea of dark clouds, lightning flashing intermittently, illuminating the chaotic scene.

Balendin felt a chill run down his spine. The planet's instability was palpable, the very air charged with a sense of foreboding. He exchanged a glance with Martin/Aurelius, whose face mirrored his own apprehension.

"We need to move quickly," Xavier said, his voice cutting through the tension. "The longer we stay here, the greater the risk of being detected."

They set off towards the coordinates Liber had provided, their steps careful and deliberate. The ground beneath them seemed to pulse with energy, each step sending ripples through the unstable terrain.

As they approached their destination, the full extent of Icarus's plans became clear. The Vortixians had constructed massive structures around the vortexes, harnessing their energy for nefarious purposes. It was a scene of industrial chaos, the machinery humming with a dark energy that permeated the air.

Chapter 18

The Vortixians were on high alert, their sensors detecting the fast-approaching multi-able spaceships from different ends of the universe. Panic and anger coursed through their ranks as they realized the scale of the impending assault. They had underestimated the resolve and unity of their enemies, and now they faced the consequences.

In the command center, the Vortixian leaders barked orders, their faces twisted with fear and rage. They knew that the arrival of these ships meant only one thing: a full-scale invasion. The air was thick with tension as they prepared for the inevitable confrontation.

Meanwhile, Balendin, Martin/Aurelius, Isabella, Xander, Xavier, and King Orion had successfully used the vortex device to travel to Zamathia Vortex undetected. The journey through the vortex had been harrowing, but they had emerged on the other side with their resolve intact.

The device had worked flawlessly, creating a temporary rift that had allowed them to bypass the Vortixian defenses. They found themselves in a secluded area, hidden from the prying eyes of their enemies.

Balendin took a moment to steady himself, the weight of their mission pressing heavily on his shoulders. "We need to move quickly and quietly," he said, his voice low but firm. "We have to find Sereena and stop Icarus before it's too late."

Xavier nodded, his face set with determination. "Let's split up. We can cover more ground that way."

They divided into smaller groups, each heading in a different direction. The atmosphere was tense, every step filled with the possibility of discovery. The dark clouds above seemed to press down on them, the air thick with a sense of impending doom.

As they navigated the treacherous landscape, they encountered pockets of Vortixian resistance. The battles were fierce but brief, their resolve and unity carrying them through each skirmish. The Vortixians, despite their fear and anger, fought with a desperation born of knowing their time was running out.

Balendin's heart pounded in his chest as they neared the central structure where Sereena was being held. The air crackled with energy, the vortexes around them pulsing with a dark light. He knew they were close, the urgency of their mission driving him forward.

Aurelius's voice broke the tension. "You know, I never imagined I'd be storming an alien stronghold on a planet filled with unstable vortexes. It's almost like a bad sci-fi movie."

Leo chuckled softly, his eyes scanning the surroundings. "Just wait until we write the memoirs. No one will believe half of what we've been through."

Their moment of humor was a welcome respite, a reminder of the camaraderie that bound them together. They pressed on; their determination unwavering.

Finally, they reached the entrance to the central structure. The door was heavily guarded, but their combined skills and strategic planning allowed them to breach the defenses. As they entered the building, the air grew colder, the sense of foreboding intensifying.

Inside, they found Sereena, her eyes filled with relief and hope as she saw them. Balendin rushed to her side, his heart bursting with emotion. "Sereena, we're here. We're going to get you out of here."

Tears filled her eyes as she embraced him. "I knew you would come," she whispered, her voice filled with gratitude and love.

As they prepared to make their escape, the ground beneath them trembled, the instability of the planet reaching a critical point. They knew they had to move quickly, the window of opportunity rapidly closing.

With Sereena safely with them, they made their way back to the vortex device, their hearts pounding with a mix of fear and determination. The journey back was fraught with danger, the Vortixians growing more desperate in their attempts to stop them.

But their resolve was unbreakable. They fought with everything they had, their love for each other and their determination to protect their world driving them forward. Finally, they reached the vortex device, activating it just as the ground beneath them began to give way.

The transition back to Xyphoria Prime was a blur of colors and sounds, the fabric of reality bending and twisting around them. When they emerged on the other side, they found themselves back in the palace, the familiar surroundings a stark contrast to the chaos they had just escaped.

They were greeted with cheers and tears of joy, the relief and gratitude of their friends and allies palpable. Balendin held Sereena close, his heart filled with love and relief. They had succeeded. They had brought her home.

As they stood together, surrounded by the people they loved, they knew that their journey was far from over. There would be more challenges ahead, but they would face them together, united by love and determination.

The atmosphere in the throne room was heavy with the aftermath of their recent victory. The joy of Sereena's rescue was tempered by the knowledge that the threat of Icarus still loomed large. Xavier stood apart from the others, his face set with a determination that hadn't been seen before.

"I have to go back and destroy Icarus so he can't hurt anyone again," Xavier said, his voice firm but carrying an undertone of sorrow.

Aurelius turned to him, his eyes wide with concern. "Xavier, you can't do this alone. It's too dangerous."

Balendin stepped forward, his face etched with worry. "We just got through one battle. Don't go rushing into another. We need you here."

Xander nodded in agreement. "You don't have to do this by yourself. We can find another way."

Xavier's usual sarcasm slipped through, a bitter edge to his words. "And what? Wait for Icarus to come to us? No, he needs to be stopped now, and I'm the only one who can do it."

Leo watched him closely, his eyes reflecting a deep understanding of his pain. "Why now, Xavier? What's driving you?"

Xavier took a deep breath, his emotions raw. "Icarus... he took everything from me. My home, my people... my wife." His voice broke slightly, the pain of the memory evident. "Her name was Elara. She was beautiful, strong, everything to me. And I killed her."

The room fell silent as Xavier's confession hung in the air. "She was caught in the crossfire of a battle Icarus started. I tried to save her, but I couldn't. She died because of me."

Tears welled in Xavier's eyes as he continued. "I've carried that guilt for so long. I couldn't protect her. I couldn't stop him then, but I can now. I must."

Balendin placed a hand on Xavier's shoulder, his eyes filled with sympathy. "We understand your pain, but please, don't do this alone."

Xavier shook his head, a sad smile on his lips. "This is something I have to do. For Elara. For everyone I've lost."

With that, Xavier activated the vortex device, the portal shimmering into existence. He stepped through without looking back, his resolve unwavering.

The transition was as disorienting as ever, the colours and sounds a chaotic swirl. When Xavier emerged on the other side, he found himself back on the unstable terrain of Zamathia Vortex. The dark clouds roiled above, casting an eerie light over the landscape.

His thoughts were a maelstrom of emotions—grief, anger, determination. He had stored his anger for so long, and now it fueled his every step. He would find Icarus and end this once and for all.

Xavier navigated the treacherous landscape with purpose, his mind focused on the task ahead. He knew where Icarus would be, in the heart of the Vortixian stronghold. As he approached, he could see the dark energy pulsing around the structure, a testament to Icarus's power.

Inside, the air was thick with tension. Xavier moved silently through the corridors until he found Icarus in a grand chamber, surrounded by swirling vortexes of energy. The sight of him ignited a fury in Xavier that burned hotter than ever.

"Icarus!" Xavier's voice echoed through the chamber.

Icarus turned, a smug smile on his face. "Ah, Xavier. I was wondering when you'd show up. Come to join the winning side?"

Xavier's eyes blazed with anger. "This ends now. You've caused enough pain and destruction."

Icarus laughed, a cold, mocking sound. "Do you really think you can stop me? You're just as much a pawn in this game as the rest."

The words hit Xavier like a physical blow, but he stood firm. "You kidnapped Aurelius when he was a child and wiped his memory when we came looking for him, manipulated a man named Aeneas to do your bidding. All to create chaos. But it ends here."

Icarus's smile faded, replaced by a look of dark intensity. "Yes, I did. And it was so easy. Men like Aeneas are always looking for someone to follow. But you, Xavier, you were always too stubborn to be useful."

The battle erupted with a ferocity that shook the very ground. Xavier summoned all his magical power, his anger and grief fueling his attacks. Icarus countered with dark energy, their clash lighting up the chamber in a dazzling display of power.

For a moment, Xavier feared he was losing. Icarus's strength was overwhelming, his dark energy pushing Xavier to the brink. But then he thought of Elara, of all the lives at stake, and found a renewed strength within himself.

With a roar of defiance, Xavier surged forward, his magic blazing brighter than ever. He channeled all his power into a final, devastating attack. The energy crackled and surged, enveloping Icarus and shattering his defenses.

Icarus's scream of rage and pain echoed through the chamber as the dark energy dissipated. Xavier stood over him, his chest heaving with exertion, his eyes burning with a fierce determination.

"It's over, Icarus," Xavier said, his voice trembling with emotion. "You won't hurt anyone ever again."

With a final, decisive strike, Xavier ended Icarus's reign of terror. The dark energy that had permeated the chamber faded, leaving only silence in its wake.

Xavier fell to his knees, the weight of his actions crashing down on him. The anger and grief he had carried for so long began to lift, replaced by a sense of peace. He had avenged Elara, protected his friends, and stopped a great evil.

As he activated the vortex device to return to Xyphoria Prime, Xavier felt a profound sense of relief. The journey back was a blur, his mind filled with thoughts of those he had fought for and the hope that now, finally, they could find peace.

When he emerged back in the palace, he was greeted with cheers and tears of joy. His friends and allies surrounded him, their relief and gratitude palpable. Balendin, Martin, Leo, Xander, and King Orion embraced him, their eyes reflecting their appreciation and under-standing.

"You did it," Aurelius said, his voice filled with awe.

Xavier nodded, a weary smile on his face. "It's over. Icarus is gone."

As they celebrated their victory, Xavier felt a sense of closure. The journey had been long and painful, but he had found redemption. He had avenged Elara and protected those he loved. And now, finally, he could begin to heal.

Chapter 20

Balendin stood on the palace balcony, gazing out over the serene landscape of Xyphoria Prime. The recent events had been harrowing, but now, with Sereena safe, he felt a sense of peace returning to his heart. He needed to spend some time alone with her, away from the chaos and turmoil that had surrounded them.

He found Sereena in the garden, her presence a beacon of light in the verdant surroundings. She looked up as he approached, a soft smile lighting up her face. The love and relief in her eyes mirrored his own feelings.

"Balendin," she whispered, stepping into his arms. "It's finally over."

He held her close, the warmth of her body soothing the lingering anxiety in his heart. "Yes, it is. And now, we can finally have some time to ourselves."

They decided to retreat to their secret place, a hidden grove deep within the forest that surrounded the palace. It was a place known only to them, a sanctuary where they could escape the demands of their roles and be simply themselves. As they walked hand in hand through the forest, the sunlight filtering through the trees cast a dappled glow on the path ahead.

The grove was as beautiful as ever, a small clearing surrounded by towering trees and filled with wildflowers of every colour. A gentle stream ran through it, its clear waters sparkling in the sunlight. It was a place of peace and beauty, a reflection of the love they shared.

Balendin led Sereena to their favourite spot by the stream, a soft patch of grass where they often sat together. He watched her as she settled down, her eyes closed and a contented smile on her lips. The sight filled his heart with a fierce, protective love.

"Sereena," he said softly, sitting beside her and taking her hand in his. "I've missed this. Just being here with you, away from everything."

She opened her eyes and looked at him, her gaze filled with tenderness. "I've missed it too. It feels like it's been forever since we could just be together like this."

He leaned in, his lips brushing against her forehead. "I love you, Sereena. More than anything in this world."

She smiled, her eyes shining with love. "I love you too, Balendin. You've always been my strength, my hope."

Their lips met in a gentle kiss, the world around them fading away. It was a kiss filled with all the emotions they had held back, a promise of love and devotion. Balendin felt a deep longing as he kissed her, wanting to feel her soft lips against his forever.

The intimacy between them grew, their kisses becoming more passionate, more urgent. Balendin's hands roamed over her body, savouring the feel of her soft skin. He felt her responding to his touch, her breath quickening as their desire for each other intensified.

They lost themselves in each other, their love a force that transcended the chaos and danger they had faced. It was a moment of pure connection, a reminder of the bond that had carried them through the darkest of times.

After a while, they lay together on the grass, their bodies entwined. Balendin felt a sense of contentment, a deep peace that came from being with the woman he loved. He looked at Sereena, her face glowing with happiness, and knew that he wanted to spend the rest of his life with her.

"Sereena," he began, his voice trembling slightly with emotion. "There's something I've been meaning to ask you."

She looked up at him, her eyes filled with curiosity and love. "What is it, Balendin?"

He took a deep breath, his heart pounding in his chest. "I know this might not be the perfect moment, and I know I'm not always the most eloquent person, but... will you marry me?"

There was a moment of silence as Sereena processed his words. Then a brilliant smile spread across her face, her eyes filling with tears of joy. "Yes, Balendin. Yes, I will marry you."

Balendin let out a breath he hadn't realized he was holding, a wave of relief and happiness washing over him. "You will?" he asked, a grin spreading across his face.

She laughed, the sound pure and joyous. "Of course I will. I can't imagine my life without you."

They kissed again; a kiss filled with the promise of a shared future. Balendin felt a sense of completeness, a feeling that everything was finally falling into place. They had faced so much together, and now, they could look forward to a life filled with love and happiness.

As they lay together in their secret grove, surrounded by the beauty of nature and the love they shared, Balendin knew that they could face anything the future held. With Sereena by his side, he felt invincible, ready to embrace whatever challenges came their way.

The sun began to set, casting a warm, golden light over the grove. They watched the sky change colors, their hands intertwined, their hearts beating in sync. It was a perfect moment, a memory they would cherish forever.

"Thank you, Balendin," Sereena whispered, her head resting on his shoulder. "For everything. For loving me, for protecting me, for being my rock."

He kissed the top of her head, his heart swelling with love. "I'll always be here for you, Sereena. Always."

As the stars began to appear in the night sky, they lay together, talking about their dreams, their hopes, and the life they would build together. The grove, their secret sanctuary, was a place of beginnings, a place where their love had flourished and would continue to grow.

Balendin felt a sense of gratitude, a profound appreciation for the woman beside him and the journey they had shared. They had been through so much, but their love had only grown stronger. And now, as they looked to the future, he knew that they would face it together, united by an unbreakable bond.

The night air was cool and refreshing, filled with the sounds of the forest and the gentle flow of the stream. Balendin and Sereena lay side by side, their hearts full, their spirits lifted. They had found their way back to each other, and nothing could tear them apart.

As they drifted off to sleep, wrapped in each other's arms, Balendin whispered a silent promise to himself: to cherish every moment, to love Sereena with all his heart, and to build a life filled with joy and happiness. It was a promise he knew he would keep, a promise that would guide them through the rest of their lives.

As the night deepened, the stars shone brightly above the grove, casting a soft, ethereal light over the tranquil scene. Balendin and Sereena remained entwined in each other's arms, their hearts beating as one. The intimacy they shared was profound, a testament to the love that had grown and flourished despite the many challenges they had faced.

Balendin stroked Sereena's hair, his fingers gently tracing the strands as he held her close. "You know," he said softly, breaking the comfortable silence, "I used to dream about moments like this. Just the two of us, away from the world, in our own little paradise."

Sereena lifted her head to look at him, her eyes shimmering with emotion. "Me too, Balendin. I always felt safest when I was with you. You make me feel like everything will be alright, no matter what happens."

He smiled, leaning down to press a tender kiss to her lips. "I promise I'll always be here for you. We've faced so much together, and we've come out stronger. I know we can handle anything life throws at us."

They talked late into the night, sharing their hopes and dreams for the future. Sereena spoke of the family she hoped they would have the children who would grow up knowing the love and strength of their parents. Balendin's heart swelled with pride and love as he listened to her, imagining the life they would build together.

"I want our children to know the beauty of Xyphoria Prime," Sereena said, her voice filled with a quiet passion. "I want them to grow up exploring places like this grove, to understand the importance of nature and the world around them."

Balendin nodded, his eyes fixed on her with unwavering devotion. "And I want them to know the strength of love and unity. To see how powerful we can be when we stand together."

As the first light of dawn began to creep over the horizon, they reluctantly prepared to leave their secret grove. They knew they had responsibilities waiting for them, but the time they had spent together had rejuvenated their spirits and strengthened their bond.

On their way back to the palace, they held hands, their fingers intertwined. Balendin couldn't help but steal glances at Sereena, marveling at her beauty and the lightness in her step. He felt a deep sense of gratitude for the woman by his side, the love of his life.

When they arrived back at the palace, they were greeted by the sight of their family, friends and allies preparing for the day ahead. Balendin felt a renewed sense of purpose, a determination to protect the future he and Sereena had envisioned.

As the days passed, Balendin and Sereena made a point of carving out moments for themselves amidst the busyness of their lives. They returned to their secret grove whenever they could, finding solace and peace in their private sanctuary. Each visit strengthened their connection, deepening the love they shared.

One evening, as they sat by the stream, Sereena leaned into Balendin's embrace, a contented sigh escaping her lips. "Do you remember the day we found this place?" she asked, her voice filled with nostalgia.

Balendin smiled, pressing a kiss to her temple. "How could I forget? We were exploring the forest, and you insisted on going off the beaten path. I thought we'd get lost, but you led us straight here."

Sereena laughed softly. "I just had a feeling about this place. And I was right, wasn't I?"

"You were," he agreed, his eyes filled with admiration. "This place has become a part of us, a symbol of our love and our journey toget her.".

Their family, friends and allies noticed the change in them, the way they moved with a newfound confidence and joy. It was clear to everyone that Balendin and Sereena were meant to be together, their love a shining example of what was possible when two hearts truly connected.

As they prepared for their wedding, the palace was filled with excitement and anticipation. The ceremony would be a celebration of their love, a testament to the journey they had shared and the future they would build together.

On the day of their wedding, the grove was transformed into a magical setting, filled with flowers and lights. Their friends and family gathered to witness their union, their hearts filled with joy and love.

As Balendin and Sereena stood before their loved ones, exchanging vows and promises, the world seemed to fade away, leaving only the two of them. It was a moment of pure, unadulterated happiness, a culmination of their love and commitment. Martin/ Aurelius was best man, Xavier did the ceremony, Caius was the ring bearer and Sereena`s father King Orion gave his daughter away with a glancing look at Balendin which made him nervous and then winked at his son in law.

When they kissed, sealing their vows, the grove erupted in cheers and applause. The love that had been nurtured in their secret place had blossomed into something beautiful and everlasting.

As they danced under the stars, surrounded by the people they loved, Balendin and Sereena knew that their journey was just beginning. They had faced many challenges, but their love had carried them through. And now, as they looked to the future, they knew that they could face anything together.

Their hearts were full, their spirits lifted, and their love a beacon of hope and joy. They had found their way back to each other, and nothing could tear them apart.

To them the grove, their secret sanctuary, would always be a place of beginnings, a place where their love had flourished and would continue to grow. And as they danced under the stars, they knew that they were exactly where they were meant to be together, in love, and ready to face the future hand in hand.

Chapter 21

The days turned into weeks, and the weeks into months. Balendin and Sereena's love continued to grow, their connection deepening with each passing moment. They faced their challenges with grace and determination, always finding their way back to each other.

Aurelius was a constant visitor he would often say Xyphoria Prime their home and making it permanently with Catherine and Caius was good choice. Balendin was grateful for that as he had his brother back for good.

Friends and family remained a constant source of support, their bonds strengthened by the trials they had faced. Together, they built a community of love and resilience, a testament to the power of unity and the strength of the human spirit.

They know as the years passed, that their love story will become a legend, a beacon of hope and inspiration for all who heard it. They had faced darkness and emerged stronger for it, their love a shining example of what was possible when two hearts truly connected and their secret grove remained a place of magic and beauty, a symbol of their journey and the love that had carried them through. And as they looked to the future, they knew that their love would continue to guide them, lighting the way for generations to come.

The seasons changed, bringing new life and beauty to Xyphoria Prime. Balendin and Sereena continued to grow closer, their love deepening with each passing day. They cherished the moments they spent together, whether they were working to improve their world or simply enjoying each other's company.

Their secret grove became a sanctuary not just for them, but also for their friends and family. It was a place where they could gather, share stories, and find solace in the beauty of nature. The grove, with its tranquil stream and vibrant flowers, was a symbol of the love and unity that bound them all together.

One afternoon, Balendin and Sereena decided to take a break from their duties and spend some time alone in their special place. The sun was high in the sky, casting a warm glow over the landscape as they walked hand in hand through the forest.

When they reached the grove, they settled down on the soft grass by the stream. The sound of the water flowing gently over the rocks was soothing, a reminder of the peace they had fought so hard to achieve.

"I love this place," Sereena said, leaning her head on Balendin's shoulder. "It's like our own little paradise."

Balendin smiled, wrapping his arm around her. "It is. And it's even more special because I get to share it with you."

They sat in comfortable silence for a while, enjoying the beauty of their surroundings. Balendin watched as a pair of birds flitted through the trees, their cheerful songs filling the air. It was moments like these that reminded him of how fortunate he was to have Sereena by his side.

"I've been thinking," Sereena said softly, breaking the silence. "About our future. About the family we want to build."

Balendin turned to look at her, his eyes filled with love and curiosity. "What about it?"

She smiled, her eyes sparkling. "I want us to start our family soon. I want to bring new life into this world; to share the love we have with our children."

His heart swelled with happiness at her words. "I want that too, Sereena. More than anything."

They kissed, a promise of the life they would create together. The prospect of starting a family filled them both with excitement and joy, a new chapter in their journey together.

As the sun began to set, casting a golden light over the grove, they talked about their dreams and aspirations for their future children. They imagined the adventures they would have, the lessons they would teach, and the love they would share.

"We'll show them this place," Balendin said, his voice filled with warmth. "Our secret grove. It will be a part of their lives, just as it's been a part of ours."

Sereena nodded, her eyes shining with tears of happiness. "And we'll teach them about love and unity, about the strength that comes from standing together."

Their dreams for the future were filled with hope and promise, a testament to the love that had carried them through so many challenges. They knew that their journey was far from over, but they were ready to face whatever came their way, hand in hand.

The months that followed were filled with joy and anticipation. Balendin and Sereena continued their work, dedicating themselves to improving the lives of their people and building a better world. They found strength in each other, their love a constant source of inspiration and resilience.

Their friends and family remained by their side, supporting them through every challenge and celebrating every triumph. The bonds they had forged were unbreakable, a testament to the power of love and unity.

As the evening emerge, they sat together in the grove, Sereena placed a hand on her growing belly, a soft smile on her lips. "Can you believe it, Balendin? We're going to be parents."

Balendin's heart swelled with pride and love as he looked at her. "I can believe it. And I can't wait to meet our child. To share this beautiful world with them."

The prospect of becoming parents filled them with a sense of purpose and excitement. They knew that their lives were about to change in the most wonderful way, and they were ready to embrace the adventure ahead.

The days turned into weeks, they prepared for the arrival of their child, their love for each other growing stronger with each passing moment. They knew that their journey was just beginning, and they were ready to face whatever challenges came their way.

The day finally arrived when Sereena went into labor. The palace was abuzz with anticipation as their friends and family gathered to support them. Balendin stayed by Sereena's side, holding her hand and offering words of encouragement as she brought their child into the world.

When the cries of their newborn filled the air, Balendin felt a rush of emotions joy, relief, and an overwhelming sense of love. He looked at Sereena, her face radiant with happiness, and knew that their lives had been forever changed.

"It's a boy," the Life spring Guardian announced, placing the tiny bundle in Sereena's arms.

Tears streamed down Balendin's face as he looked at his son, his heart swelling with love and pride. "He's perfect," he whispered, his voice choked with emotion. "Just like his mother."

Sereena smiled up at him, her eyes filled with tears of joy. "We did it, Balendin. We created this beautiful life together."

They held their son close, their hearts overflowing with love and gratitude. It was a moment of pure happiness, a culmination of their journey and a promise of the future they would build together.

As they introduced their son to their friends and family, the joy and love that filled the room were palpable. Their child was a symbol of hope and new beginnings, a testament to the strength of their love and the unity of their community.

Aurelius stood up he felt so proud and hugged his brother, "Congratulations! Now Caius has a cousin to play with."

In the days that followed, Balendin and Sereena settled into their new roles as parents, finding joy in the simple moments of their everyday lives. They watched their son grow, marvelling at each new milestone and cherishing every moment they spent together.

They sat by their favorite place by the stream, watching their son play in the grass, Balendin took Sereena's hand in his, his heart full. "I love you, Sereena. More than words can ever express. Thank you for this beautiful life we've created together."

Sereena leaned her head on his shoulder, her eyes filled with love. "I love you too, Balendin. And I'm so grateful for every moment we share. Our journey has been incredible, and I can't wait to see what the future holds."

They kissed, a gentle promise of the love and commitment that would carry them through whatever challenges lay ahead. Their hearts were united, their love an unbreakable bond that would guide them through the rest of their lives.

As they looked to the future, they knew that they could face anything together. Their love had carried them through darkness and brought them into the light, and it would continue to be their guiding star. With their son by their side and their friends and family supporting them, they were ready to embrace the adventures that awaited them.

Chapter 22

Following the birth of Balendin's and Sereena's son, Aurelius, Catherine and Caius settled very quickly into life on Xyphoria Prime. Life was perfect. The verdant landscapes, the crystal-clear rivers, and the vibrant cities provided a serene backdrop for their new beginning. The air was fresher, the skies clearer, and there was an undeniable sense of tranquility that enveloped them.

The decision to live permanently on Xyphoria Prime had been a pivotal one, arrived at after much deliberation and heartfelt discussions. Catherine and Aurelius had weighed their options carefully, considering not just their happiness but the future of their children as well. They had once been hesitant, torn between their love for Earth and the promising new life that Xyphoria Prime offered. But as they observed the joy on Caius's face and the contentment in Catherine's eyes, they knew they had made the right choice.

Catherine often found herself reflecting on their journey. Sitting by the window of their new home, she watched Caius play in the garden, his laughter a melody that filled her heart with warmth. The lush gardens of Xyphoria Prime filled with exotic flora and vibrant colors, provided the perfect playground for their son. She marveled at how quickly he adapted, his curiosity and enthusiasm for their new world a constant source of delight.

Life on Xyphoria Prime was not just about beautiful scenery; it was about the sense of community and belonging they had found. Catherine and Aurelius quickly integrated into the local society, forming bonds that felt as strong as those they had left behind. They were welcomed with open arms, the people of Xyphoria embracing them as family.

Aurelius, ever the adventurer, found endless opportunities to explore and engage with the environment. He had joined the Xyphorian Council of the Court, working closely with to ensure that Xyphoria continued to thrive. His passion for governance and his knack for diplomacy made him an invaluable asset, and his efforts were deeply appreciated by the Xyphorians.

Meanwhile, Catherine discovered her own calling. She became involved in education, sharing her knowledge and experience with the children of Xyphoria. Her classroom was a vibrant space, filled with laughter and learning, and she found immense satisfaction in nurturing the next generation. Her students adored her, and she quickly became a beloved figure in the community.

Caius, their son, was the true joy of their lives. He had inherited Aurelius's strong will and Catherine's gentle heart, a combination that made him both determined and compassionate. Every day was an adventure for him, and he approached each one with wide-eyed wonder. He had quickly made friends, his cheerful nature endearing him to everyone he met. Whether it was playing with the local children or exploring the natural wonders of Xyphoria Prime, Caius was thriving.

Catherine and Aurelius often spoke of how content they were with their life. "This place feels like home," Catherine would say, her voice filled with emotion. "It's everything we dreamed of and more."

Aurelius would nod in agreement, his eyes soft with affection. "And seeing Caius so happy... it makes everything worthwhile."

Xander, too, was a constant presence in their lives. As the patriarch of the family, he had always dreamed of a future where his descendants could live in peace and prosperity. Now, seeing Caius grow up in such a loving and nurturing environment, his heart swelled with pride. He took an active role in his grandson's upbringing, teaching him the values and traditions that had been passed down through generations.

Caius adored his grandfather, often following him around and listening intently to his stories. Xander's tales of bravery and wisdom captivated him, and he soaked up every lesson like a sponge. "One day, you'll be a great leader, just like your father, Uncle and grandfather," Xander would say, his voice filled with pride. "Always remember the importance of kindness and courage."

These words resonated deeply with Aurelius. He looked up to Xander with immense admiration, eager to make him proud. The bond between them was a testament to the strength of family and the love that bound them all together.

The days passed in a blissful blur of happiness and fulfilment. Catherine often found herself overwhelmed with gratitude for the life they had built. She would watch Caius playing in the garden, his laughter echoing through the air, and feel a deep sense of peace. "This is what we've always wanted," she would say to Aurelius, her voice filled with emotion. "A place where we can be happy, where our son can grow up surrounded by love."

Aurelius would take her hand, his eyes reflecting the same contentment. "We've made the right choice, Catherine. This is our home."

The community of Xyphoria Prime became an extended family for them. The people would drop by with freshly baked goods, children played together in the sprawling gardens, and there was a palpable sense of unity that brought everyone closer. Festivities were frequent, with celebrations of local traditions and new beginnings, each one strengthening the bonds within the community.

One evening, as the family gathered for dinner, Catherine looked around the table at the faces of those she loved. Balendin and Sereena, Xander, Aurelius, and little Caius each one a vital piece of her heart. The conversation flowed easily, punctuated by laughter and shared memories. It was in these moments that Catherine felt the true meaning of home.

Aurelius, watching his son interact with his grandfather, felt an overwhelming sense of pride. Caius was growing up to be a kind, intelligent, and curious young boy. He saw the best parts of himself and Catherine in their son and knew that they had made the right decision in choosing to raise him on Xyphoria Prime. "Caius is thriving here," he said to Catherine, his voice filled with emotion. "He's happy, and so are we."

Catherine smiled, her eyes glistening with tears of joy. "Yes, he is. And so are we."

As the night drew to a close, Catherine took a moment to herself, stepping outside to gaze at the stars. The sky above Xyphoria Prime was a breathtaking canvas of twinkling lights, a reminder of the vastness of the universe and the beauty of their small corner within it. She felt a deep sense of connection to this place, to the land and the people who had become her family.

Aurelius joined her, wrapping his arms around her and resting his chin on her shoulder. "What are you thinking about?" he asked softly.

Catherine leaned into him; her heart full. "Just how perfect everything is. Our family, our home... it's more than I ever dreamed."

Aurelius pressed a kiss to her temple. "And it's all because of you, Catherine. Your love and strength have made this possible."

Tears of happiness filled her eyes as she turned to face him. "And yours, Aurelius. Together, we've built something beautiful."

As they stood there, wrapped in each other's arms, Catherine felt a profound sense of gratitude. Life on Xyphoria Prime was more than perfect; it was a dream come true. She knew there would be challenges ahead, but with Aurelius by her side and their family united, she was ready to face anything.

The following days were filled with a sense of purpose and fulfillment. Catherine continued her work teaching the children, her passion for teaching inspiring her children. Aurelius, ever the diligent leader, made significant strides in his role on the Xyphorian Council along with his brother Balendin, their innovative ideas and diplomatic skills helping to shape the future of their home.

Caius, their bright and curious son, continued to thrive. His days were filled with learning and adventure, his boundless energy a constant source of joy for his parents. He excelled in his studies, his natural curiosity driving him to explore the world around him. The Mentors often remarked on his intelligence and kindness, qualities that made him a beloved figure among his peers.

Xander, ever the proud grandfather, took every opportunity to spend time with Caius. He taught him the traditions and values of their family, sharing stories of their ancestors and instilling in him a deep sense of honor and duty. "You are part of a long line of strong and noble men," he would say, his voice filled with pride. "Never forget where you come from, and always strive to be the best version of yourself."

Caius listened intently, soaking up his grandfather's wisdom like a sponge. He admired Xander greatly and wanted nothing more than to make him proud. "I will, Grandfather," he would say, his young face serious and determined. "I promise."

The bond between Caius and Xander was a source of great joy for the entire family. Seeing them together, Catherine and Aurelius often felt a deep sense of pride and gratitude. Their son was growing up surrounded by love and wisdom, his future bright and filled with promise.

As the seasons changed and the years passed, the family's bond only grew stronger. Catherine and Aurelius often reflected on their journey, marvelling at how far they had come. Their decision to make Xyphoria Prime their home had been the right one, a choice that had brought them happiness and fulfillment beyond their wildest dreams.

One day, as Catherine and Aurelius watched Caius play in the garden, they couldn't help but smile. Life on Xyphoria Prime was perfect, a testament to their love and determination. They had built a home filled with joy and laughter, a place where their son could grow and thrive.

As the sun set, casting a golden glow over their home, Catherine leaned into Aurelius, her heart full. "We've created something beautiful," she said softly.

Aurelius nodded, his eyes filled with love. "And we'll continue to do so, every day. This is our home, our family, and our future."

In that moment, Catherine knew that they were exactly where they were meant to be. Xyphoria Prime was not just a place; it was a symbol of their love, their resilience, and their commitment to each other. And as they stood together, watching their son play, they knew that their future was bright, filled with endless possibilities and boundless joy.